# LUCAS' OMEGA

Creekside Township Rivals

Book 1

JT Fader

Published by Steambath Press
A Creekside Township Rivals Romance

Paperback published December 2023
ISBN-13: 978-1-998008-40-7

# Chapter One | Adam

Creekside Township was as sleepy as I had hoped it would be. From where I was parked, you could see from one end of the downtown core to the other. A single street lined with quaint stores and houses. I was almost surprised there weren't wooden sidewalks. There was a real yester-year feeling to the place. I climbed out of my truck and sniffed the air. There was the faint scent of local wolves who had crossed the street moments before I arrived. One alpha. Two omegas.

I closed my eyes. It was going to take a bit to get used to—the absolute silence in my mind. Fifty miles from my previous home, my connection with my wolf pack had fallen deathly quiet.

I'd had to pull my truck over for a solid thirty minutes while I broke down in tears. Sobbing had turned to crying had turned to sniffling. Bleary-eyed, I'd started driving again.

They were the pack of my birth. Leaving them had been the hardest decision of my life but I couldn't stand being connected with my ex-mate any longer. Hearing the constant communication between my pack and him and his new mate had sent me into a deep depression.

I was doing this for my mental health. I needed to pull away. Start a new life somewhere different and quiet. There were two packs in the township of Creekside. They'd had over sixty years of peace according to the stories. On the territory maps, the two regions showed as separated by the creek, but they both used Creekside as their hub and by all accounts, it was an agreement that worked. They coexisted alongside each other without any major skirmishes.

Their politics didn't interest me other than it would be a serene place to start fresh. I had no intention of approaching either pack to be brought into their fold. I was done with all that. Being telepathically connected with other wolves was comforting but it was also exhausting. There was so much chatter. I had always felt obliged to listen in case something important was said.

All that information typically only served to increase the frequency of my chronic anxiety attacks. I'd been diagnosed with an anxiety disorder back in my 20s. Now in my early 30s, I wasn't any better at coping. Stubborn—I had refused any kind of medication. This meant my mind was constantly on high alert, but as a shifter, needing human pharmaceuticals made me feel weak.

I was anything but.

It was risky coming into town as a lone wolf, but I felt prepared to defend myself. I was an Omega, but I was strong and aggressive. I'd taken down a few Alphas in my time who had challenged me. Or shown too much unwanted interest in me. I was fussy about who I rutted with.

I slammed the door of my truck and looked down at my two duffel bags. They contained the entirety of my personal belongings. I set them on the ground and pulled out my phone. As expected, there were zero bars. There probably wasn't a cell tower for miles. Luckily, I had anticipated the lack of service and typed the directions in the Notes app on my phone to the boarding house where I'd be staying. I'd be relying on their Wi-Fi to conduct my business.

The house was located halfway down the street on the right. There hadn't been any parking out front. I looked in the stores as I passed by them. I was pleased to see a hardware store. I needed to pick up a few things before starting my electrician company in a new location.

That was the plan. Come into Creekside and see if I could pick up some odd jobs to start building my reputation. I had some money saved up. I would be fine without regular work for almost six months. Hopefully, that would be enough time.

It hadn't been my first choice—to be an electrician. I had wanted to be a graphic artist. But I soon discovered that particular career choice didn't always pay the bills.

My sire had been an electrician. He had died when I was ten and I had decided to honor him by pursuing the same career. It had come easily to me. Twelve years later, I was still at it. There was satisfaction in it. A methodical rhythm of stringing and clipping. The colored wires winding their way through open walls almost fulfilled my thirst for artistic expression.

Installing fixtures wasn't as much fun. Tedious would be the word, but that task made up much of my billable time. New builds were often taken on by larger companies. I was one guy. I'd never employed anyone else to help me out. I preferred the solitude.

With a slight flutter filling my gut, I walked toward the boarding house. I was met by a few humans walking in the opposite direction. Their scent was familiar but unpleasant. Their diet which included a large variety of vegetables made them smell like rotting vegetation.

As they approached, some smiled at me and said hello. It was a small town. I was sure I had already been pegged as a stranger. I responded in kind with a forced smile and nod to protect my wild carnivorous identity. I wrinkled my nose after each of them passed by me.

Humans knew wolf shifters existed amongst them, but they barely tolerated us. They tended to be fearful of the Alphas once they figured out who they were. Omegas were a different situation. They knew where we stood in the hierarchy of a pack. They treated us accordingly. Especially when a male Omega of our species was showing as pregnant. Human males didn't carry babies.

In our world, both females and Omega males could carry pups.

Unfortunately, walking around as an unchaperoned, pregnant male Omega among humans came with a level of ridicule that made you want to not do it again. Not that I had ever experienced it. My ex-mate and I had decided we didn't want pups. Now I knew why. My mate had been waiting for his fated mate to appear. He had been biding his time with me, his chosen mate.

We'd gone as far as claiming each other, opening a telepathic connection with one another alone. That had been shredded when he claimed his new mate. But it hadn't been a complete severing of our connection. Sometimes I had caught glimmers of his communication with the man who had replaced me. Another reason I needed to leave.

Hearing him like that was too much to endure.

I had been deeply in love with my mate. I had imagined an incredible future with him. Someday deciding to have pups after all. I only agreed to start birth control because that's what he had wanted. And he was my Alpha. It was in my DNA to obey his wants and needs.

When we were in wolf form, I would often find myself bowing to him.

It was a part of me that irritated the independent side of myself. Especially, now that I was on the far end of my relationship with him. Deep down, I felt like an Alpha. I fought the impulse to obey him when I first met him and realized I was drawn to him. We should have just rutted and left it at that. Walked away before we became entangled. But he hadn't given me that option.

I had been pulled along into a relationship that felt right and wrong at the same time. Over time, I had fallen in love with him. He treated me as though I was the most precious thing to him. I had thought he loved me too. Within days of meeting his fated mate, he had dumped me.

I looked up at the boarding house windows. It was a two-story structure probably built in the early 1900s. It looked almost rickety as if the exposed beams were the only things supporting it.

I pulled open the door and immediately detected the scent of a wolf. The owner of that scent approached me; a woman likely in her early 70s. She appeared to be in charge.

"Welcome," she said. "You must be Adam."

"That I am." I smiled at her. A genuine smile. Finding a friendly wolf so early after my arrival warmed me through. Three meals each day with her was going to be pleasant. I could tell.

Plus, she'd know what to cook for me. I had been concerned about that. Asking for food heavy on the meat from a human would have likely given me away. A human finding out I was an Omega would have had me kicked out onto the street and there would have been nowhere else to go. It was the only boarding house in town. I had been lucky to secure a room.

"My name is Clara but some of the men who have been here for a while call me Mama." She rubbed my arm. "I have a lovely quiet suite for you at the back of the house."

"Thank you." I followed her up the stairs. The bare wood creaked with each step we took. She led me to a door at the end of the hallway. She unlocked and opened it. Inside was a cozy room. Big comfy bed piled high with comforters. A fair-sized round table and two chairs. And along one wall, a kitchenette. A microwave, coffee maker, toaster, dishes, and a fridge.

It was perfect.

I could set up my computer on one side of the table. Leave the other side for snacks and coffee. As a wolf, I had to take in a lot of calories. Shifting took a lot of energy and I liked to go for a run every morning in wolf form. I'd have to clear it with the two pack leaders first, running on their territory. I didn't want any interaction beyond that. It was protocol for me to introduce myself. I wanted to get my business up and running first, though. Running and introductions could wait.

"Thank you," I said to Clara. "This is going to suit me perfectly."

"May I ask why you're here?"

Directly to the point. She was a beta and would be reporting my presence to her pack. She would be expected to have gathered some information about me.

I settled my nerves. It wasn't a big deal. Just a few questions.

"I decided to move here because I needed a fresh start."

"Why?"

"Bad break-up with my chosen mate." I needed to give her enough information to supply her pack leader with the satisfaction that she had interrogated me thoroughly. I knew the drill. I couldn't be too secretive when it came to introducing myself. Having Clara ask me questions would provide me with an excuse to avoid going to see the pack leaders right away. Clara's pack leader would likely share the information with the pack across the creek from them.

Clara frowned. I needed to clarify.

"He found his fated mate."

Clara crossed her arms. "And he just left you? Had he claimed you?"

"He did … and he had."

Clara exhaled long and hard. She'd been inhaling my scent as I spoke, watching for changes in my pheromones that might indicate I was lying.

It appeared I had passed the test.

"Then you were lucky to escape him. Do you have pups together?"

"No, he didn't want any."

Clara's brow wrinkled. "He was willing to go against his pack's expectations?"

I simply nodded. That's the thing with pups. Alpha's and their Omega's are expected to breed and produce a family. Our numbers were declining. It was a responsibility most couples took seriously. Not my ex-mate. No pups and he was willing to dump his claimed Omega.

I sighed. I was exhausted from the long drive and starving.

"How are you planning to support yourself?"

More questions.

"I'm an electrician."

"We already have an electrician company in town."

I knew that but there was a housing development being built just outside town. I figured the larger company would be occupied with that project leaving me with small jobs.

"I doubt I'll compete with them. I'm just one guy."

"Lucas is not going to be happy."

"Who's Lucas?"

"The owner of Black's Electric and the leader of the East Creekside pack."

"Please assure him I'm not intending to steal any work from them. I only want to take on small jobs. The stuff he likely doesn't have time for."

"I'll let him know." Again, she rubbed my arm. "I'm sure you'll be welcome here. See how you feel about each pack and its leaders. There's no rush in picking one."

I wasn't going there with her. That I didn't want to join a pack. Lone wolves weren't unheard of, but they tended to hide themselves away in the depths of the forest.

My stomach groaned and grumbled.

Clara smiled at me. "I'm afraid you've missed dinner, but there's a restaurant a block down to the right. It's called *Growlers*. It is wolf run so they have plenty of all meat options on the menu. Not that you have a choice. It's the only restaurant in Creekside."

"Awesome. I'll unpack first and head down there. Thank you."

Clara headed through the open door and then turned to face me. "Breakfast is at 7."

"I'll be there." After she closed the door, I threw my duffel bags on the bed, slipped out of my coat, and began unpacking. There was a low dresser in the room with a clock radio on top.

I only managed to fill half of the dresser. I hadn't brought many clothes. City clothes seemed unsuitable in such a small town. I'd stand out with my seemingly night-out clothing.

Jeans and T-shirts would make up most of my wardrobe. Which was fine by me. I'd only dressed up at my ex-mate's insistence. I'd done a lot of things at his insistence.

I closed the last drawer. My tools were still in my truck. I wasn't worried about them being left there unattended.

Creekside didn't seem like a place where anyone would be breaking into trucks and stealing stuff. The county sheriff was probably an Alpha male.

Crime would be non-existent.

I put my empty duffel bags under the bed to keep them out of the way and hung up the only three hangable items I had. A dress shirt, dress pants, and a spring coat. We were in the middle of winter now, so my parka was soon pulled back onto my shoulders and rezipped.

I jogged down the stairs and out the front door.

The restaurant wasn't far away. It was nice to know I could get extra fills of meat any time of day I needed to. The three meals included in the price of my room was generous but not sufficient to maintain a wolf of my size. I was built. Muscular and tall. I towered over most wolves. Even Alphas. Many were surprised to catch my scent and realize I was an Omega. Even with my size, they were quick to put me in my place as soon as they figured it out. I didn't object—I couldn't.

The restaurant was another old structure. It had probably been a department store at some point. A large glass window met the sidewalk with a door to one side. Inside people were sitting in booths that reminded me of diners you would find in the city I had left behind.

I pulled open the door. The aroma of fried food and apple pie assaulted my senses. But also, meat. Lots of bloody meat; the scent wafted out from the back. Of course, the restaurant would cook the meat for the sake of preserving their human patronage. I was used to that.

"Sit anywhere you like," someone called out to me.

I spotted the one who had spoken as I found a seat at the counter; a male wolf bustling around calling out and collecting orders from the wide opening to the kitchen.

My cock paid attention. He was tasty. Lean lines, firm ass, almost petite, and a face that I could stare at for hours. Dark hair, gorgeous green eyes, and full kissable lips.

I breathed in the full scent of him. Omega. Not that I hadn't rutted with Omegas before. I had. As he approached, I tempered my desire to dull the scent of it. But not soon enough.

"I'm not interested," he said as he leaned on the counter.

"I'm sorry. It was a long drive to get here. My mind is wandering uncontrolled."

A smile lit up his handsome face. "I'm teasing you, Omega. You're delectable."

*Okay ... then, yum.*

I tapped the countertop. "I'm Adam."

He bit his bottom lip as he watched me. He eventually released it and leaned closer.

"I'm Jonas. And I'm off at 11."

I hadn't expected to find a partner to rut with on the first night in a new town. I wasn't sure I was up for it. I had spoken the truth about the long drive. But my inner wolf was howling in my mind. It wanted to be fed. Meat and pleasure. It was difficult to ignore.

"I'm sorry. I'm going to have to pass. I need sleep after I've eaten tonight. Not a rut."

"Pity." Jonas touched my hand. "Maybe another time. You staying in town for a while?"

"Yup. I moved here."

Jonas' eyebrows went up. "No one hardly ever moves here."

"That's why I picked Creekside. I'm looking for less hustle and bustle."

"You a big city wolf?"

"I was. Now I'm ready for something new."

"You need a job? I'm always looking for servers."

"No, I have my own business."

"Oh … you're *that* guy."

I sighed. My life story had already circulated through the pack's telepathic connection. Jonas must be in the same pack as Clara. Gone was any sense of mystery.

"Yeah. The running from my ex-mate, electrician guy," I said.

"My brother is not happy about your profession?"

*Oh, great.*

"Lucas is your brother?"

"Big brother." Jonas leaned his face on his hand, supporting himself on his elbow on the counter. "You do not want to cross him. I'd be thinking about the server position I offered you."

"Not going to happen. I'm only looking to pick up his scraps."

"You'll need to tell him that because honestly right now—he's angry."

"Tell him I'll come to see him once I get settled."

Jonas closed his eyes, then shook his head as he opened them. "Yeah, you're on your own. He's talking about gutting you."

I crossed my arms. If I'd been in wolf form, my hackles would have been up. No one threatened me. Not even an Alpha male. If he wanted to have a go at me, so be it.

"I'm not budging. My website is already set up and ready to go. And my social media ads poised. All I have to do is push the buttons to start everything in motion."

"None of the wolves will use you."

"Yes, I realize that, but there are plenty of humans in this town."

Jonas laughed, reached forward, and patted my shoulder. "Your funeral, Omega. What can I get you to eat? I have some roast or ribs … with no sides."

"Can you serve up a whole roast for me?"

"Heavy eater." Jonas winked at me. "I like that."

"I'm starving. Only brought a foil container of raw ribs to hold me while I was driving."

"Then I'll get right on that." He hesitated. "Since you might die tomorrow, are you sure you don't want to meet up with me tonight? I'll let you be the Alpha."

"Tempting, but no. I really do need sleep."

Jonas exhaled. "Okay, one roast it is." He turned from me and told the kitchen my order in a hushed voice. No need to announce I was ordering off the menu.

I looked around the restaurant. All humans. There was an empty booth in the back of the space. It would give me the privacy I needed to consume a meal of strictly meat. I wandered over to it, removed my coat, and slid along the seat until I was up against the wall. No one other than Jonas and the kitchen staff could see me. I wouldn't need to be neat and use utensils.

The roast must have been cooked, unsliced, and sitting in a warmer because Jonas had it in front of me within minutes. He set a glass of what looked to be tomato juice in front of me.

"There's bloody drippings from before we cooked the roasts mixed in there. Usually, I keep them for myself, but you look like you need it."

My stomach growled, sounding like low thunder. The wolf in me hadn't expected such a treat. My gums pulsed as my canines began to descend. I couldn't contain the soft growl as I lifted the glass from the table. I looked up at Jonas. "I appreciate this. Thank you."

"You're welcome, Omega."

Jonas wandered away as I downed the glass of juice and drippings, and then he came back with a huge stack of napkins. He set them on the table and lifted the utensils.

"I trust you won't be needing these."

I smirked at him, lifted the roast with one hand, and bit into it. The juices ran down my arm to my elbow and off the tip of my chin. That was the entirety of my answer. My canines descended further making it easier to rip into the fibrous meat. I barely noticed when Jonas walked away. My wolf was seeing red. The meat was the only important thing in my surroundings now.

Since I was distracted, Jonas would keep anyone from seeing me feeding. We were both Omegas. When it was our turn to eat, we watched out for each other in case an Alpha wolf came back for more. There was a code amongst us. A code and an understanding.

In the short time I'd been observing Jonas, I could tell he had no mate—fated or chosen, and he'd never had pups. He appeared to be younger than me, maybe late 20s. The chances of him finding his fated or chosen mate in a town so small were slim. He would have found him by now.

I finished the last of the meat and attempted to clean my hands, arms, and face with the napkins. I decided a sink was in order and headed to the restroom to tidy up. When I emerged into the small hallway, Jonas was fussing with a mop and bucket. It was a tight space.

I had to squeeze past Jonas to get out. Again, my cock perked up and Jonas gave me a knowing smile. But I'd made up my mind. I wasn't looking for a one-night rutting session with anyone tonight. Maybe I could take Jonas up on his offer if I survived the next few days.

The scent surrounding him was tempting, though.

I paid my check and winked at Jonas before I stuffed myself back into my coat and turned for the door. The temperature outside felt as though it had dropped a lot while I was eating.

If I was in wolf form, the cold wouldn't have bothered me. But in non-wolf form, the chill was biting at me. I regretted not wearing gloves as I jogged down the street to the boarding house. I tended to run hotter than humans, as all wolves did, but I was looking forward to a warm room.

I was quick to close the door behind me to keep the draft out after I stepped inside the house. I trundled up the stairs to my little room and sighed with satisfaction as the warmth of the baseboard heaters washed over me. I looked around the room. I felt at home here.

I headed straight for the table after stripping off my coat. I didn't even bother to take off my boots. There was no reason why Lucas should have a monopoly on the electrical business in this town. I wasn't going to let some Alpha intimidate me. There was room for both of us.

And if there wasn't, maybe he should watch *his* back. The idea of taking his scraps didn't seem as palatable anymore. Not since Jonas had told me Lucas wanted to gut me.

I'd show him I wasn't an Omega to be messed with.

I sat down, opened my computer, and set my business in motion.

# Chapter Two | Lucas

I paced a few steps more around the room, then turned back and barreled straight at my brother, Bryant. "He has a god-damned website." I threw up my hands. "This is war."

"Don’t be so dramatic, Lucas."

"He can't just waltz into town and set up a business without checking with me first. We have protocols for a reason. This exact reason. Competition needs to be approved."

"Clara said he was only looking to do small jobs. We're busy with the housing development. We've been turning down small jobs for weeks. There are only four of us. We're spread thin."

"That housing development isn't going to last forever. Small jobs are our meat and bones. We can't afford to lose those customers. They've been turning to us for years."

"And we've been letting them down."

"It's temporary. They know that."

"What do you want to do about it? Challenge him?"

"No. I think we can deter him from staying in town through competition alone."

"How?"

"I'm moving you off the development jobs. I want you to pick up the small jobs again. We won't be turning anyone away. This business has been in our family for three generations. I am not going to let some Omega throw our family legacy off the ancestral hunting path."

Bryant sighed.

It was annoying when he did that. He was an Alpha like me, but I was the pack leader. I expected more enthusiasm when I gave a command.

"This isn't open for discussion, Bryant."

"I know. I'm just not looking forward to it. I have a lot of rewiring old buildings and installing light fixtures and fans in my future. I apologize, Alpha for being less than thrilled."

Before I could speak again, the phone rang. It was down the hall in the office. It was annoying not having cell service when I knew most of the rest of the world had it. I had petitioned the township council to let a cell tower be erected in town, but they had refused to consider it.

Something about it being an eyesore.

Damned humans were difficult to deal with. We only had one wolf on the town council. An Omega so she wasn't much use. The humans had elected her as a token wolf. Letting her have a seat in good faith. The truth was we were far outnumbered by humans. Likely a ratio of 50:1.

I lifted the receiver of the phone tethered to the wall by a landline.

"Black's Electric."

"Yes, hello. Tanya Carmichael here. Is this Lucas?"

"Yes."

"Lucas, I was wondering if you could send someone to give me a quote on replacing and updating some of my lights."

"How many lights are we talking about?"

"Well, the old ones in the kitchen and dining area don't fit with the remodel. So, I need six recessed lights in the kitchen over the sink and counters and a new dining room chandelier-type light. I've bought everything already; I just need a quote for the installation."

"I can give you a quote for that over the phone."

"Oh, really? All right."

"It'll cost you about $1050 plus tax."

"Oh, dear. That's a lot."

"Cutting sheetrock and wiring new lighting in the kitchen will be time-consuming."

My brows couldn't help but furrow. Why was Tanya hesitating? That's what it was going to cost her. Either she wanted the lights installed or she didn't.

A low growl threatened to spill from my throat.

I knew exactly why she was hesitating.

The Omega wolf had been in town less than a week and he was attracting our customers.

"The new guy quoted me $650. I'd prefer to support your business, but I can't turn down a quote that is so much lower. Can you meet his price?"

The *new guy's* quote number would barely cover my employee's time. I paid them $120/hr. It was a four-hour job. Then there was the cost of the extra wires and light ports. When Tanya said she had already bought the light fixtures, I doubted that included the bones of the installation.

I'd be lucky to make $150.

I grunted.

It was worth $150 to take the job away from the *new guy*.

"I'll meet his price," I said.

"Oh, wonderful. I'm sorry I've put you in such a spot, but I need to watch my money. The renovation cost us quite a bit more than we had intended."

"I'm glad you checked with me before hiring him."

"Always. You've always been good to us."

I flipped through the calendar on my desk. "Does next Tuesday at 2 pm work for you?"

"Perfect. Thank you."

"All right. See you then."

I hung up the phone. Bryant would be handling this job. I didn't care if he was going to get sick of doing small jobs. We needed to stay close to our customers.

No sooner had I returned to the living room than the phone rang again.

It was Tanya.

"I'm sorry, Lucas, the new electrician, Adam, he lowered his quote to $500."

The wolf in me dipped its head, planted its feet, and growled deep and low, lips drawn back to expose its teeth. I was going to rip this Adam to shreds.

Tear into his flesh and string out his entrails kind of shreds.

I had to check myself.

I was more ornery than usual. Something in the air was disturbing me. When Jonas had come home a few nights ago, there had been a scent lingering on him that had churned up my gut.

I knew what it meant. Deep down—I knew what it meant.

"I can't go that low." Even though Bryant was my brother, he wouldn't cut me a break on his hourly rate. He didn't receive profits from the family business like I did. I ran it and worked as hard in the field as every other employee. My sire had left the business to me … not Bryant.

He only had his billable work to bring in income. Not that he had many expenses other than his ridiculously big truck and his penchant for restoring old vehicles.

Tanya sighed. "I have to go with him for this job. I'm sorry."

"Don't be sorry. He undercut me … we'll leave it at that."

I kept my voice even so as not to upset the human but inside I was raging. "Just out of curiosity, when is he coming to do your job?"

The Omega would be getting a visit. And he'd have a few things explained to him.

"Tomorrow … noon. There won't be any trouble, I hope. Is he one of your kind?"

"Adam is new in town. I'm just sending Bryant out to introduce himself."

The human made a satisfied sound.

I turned. Jonas was standing in the doorway to the office. It was impossible to get any privacy in our house. The downside to all of us three brothers living together in one place. But it was our family home. We were a pack. We felt more comfortable sticking together.

Except Carina.

Our sister had moved out when she found her fated Alpha mate. He had his own house in our pack. After they claimed each other, it made sense for her to move in with him. Theirs was an unusual situation. Our sister was an Alpha as well. Having her fated mate be another Alpha had thrown us all into a state of confusion. You heard of it happening, but it was rare.

Now she was expecting two pups, and I was thrilled to oversee our family's growth. None of us three brothers had any prospects in that regard. Not if I could manage to control myself.

Jonas looked like he wanted to speak to me.

"Thank you again, Tanya, for thinking of us. Maybe next time."

She said goodbye and I replaced the phone in the cradle.

I crossed my arms as I gave Jonas my attention. "What?"

"You're talking about Adam?"

"Yeah, he's started stealing our business already."

Jonas scowled. "He said he wasn't going to do that."

"Well, I guess he changed his mind."

Jonas followed me down the hall to the kitchen. I needed more coffee before I started my day. Both of my pack employees were at the job site already. I'd have Bryant flip through our notes of small customers and phone those we had turned away recently.

Plus, tomorrow, he'd be visiting the human's home to intimidate the Omega.

"Tell me more about him," I said to Jonas.

Jonas smiled. "So sexy."

I grunted. "You have a one-track mind. Give me something I can use."

"He's big. Alpha big. Not sure you want to mess with him."

"Are you inferring I'm not capable of putting an Omega in his place?"

"Of course, not, Alpha. I'm just saying it might take a bit of doing. I don't think he'll bow to you. He's more likely to challenge you."

That wasn't going to happen. I wouldn't be challenging the Omega. I wouldn't be going anywhere near him. I could never come face-to-face with him.

My inner wolf whined and begged me to reconsider.

"Bryant." I turned to my other brother. "Tomorrow. Tanya Carmichael's place. Noon. I want you to go down there. Introduce yourself to this Omega. Let him know he's not welcome here."

"Do you think that'll be enough?" Bryant answered. "I could rough him up a little."

"Let's start civilized. We've fought for our place among

the humans. Let's not give them a reason to fear us any more than they do already. Just convince the Omega to move along."

"No shifting?"

"Absolutely no shifting."

Bryant sighed.

*God, that's annoying.*

Jonas leaned on the kitchen counter. "I'd prefer you didn't hurt him. Pretty sure he's going to come back for me. If he hadn't been tired his first night, we would have been in full-on rut."

"God, Jonas," I said. "Why do you have to be so crude?"

"Just speaking the truth."

I didn't have time for this. I suspected Jonas had rutted with every available male wolf in town. And maybe even a few humans. I shivered. The thought of that transgression brought me close to vomiting. If there was ever a wolf who needed to find a mate, settle down, and start having pups, it was my little brother. He was annoying but also the most joyful being I'd ever encountered.

He deserved to find his fated mate.

"We should head to work," Bryant said to me.

"Yeah, me too," Jonas responded. "My new manager is a bit shaky still."

We gathered our coats, a necessity in this weather. Bryant pulled open the front door. There was a light breeze heading up from town, and I was hit with that gut-churning sensation again.

I clenched my fists. I was going to ignore it.

Trembling, I shook my head as my inner wolf screamed, *"Mate!"*

I drove with Bryant to the worksite. It was far enough outside Creekside that the intense pull to go into town subsided. I was able to focus on my work. The day went by quickly.

The drive home had me gripping the steering wheel. My inner wolf wouldn't shut up as we drove past town and up the mountain to our house.

My cock even joined in, pulsing and thickening.

I refused to turn into a carnal animal, regardless of the temptation. Especially, because I knew who it was who was causing the reaction in my body. The damned interloper. That wasn't a path I was willing to put my nose to and follow. The Omega Adam was off-limits.

My inner wolf howled, *"Fated! Mate!"*

*Shut up.*

I had no intention of taking on another mate. I had lost one I loved desperately. My chosen mate and our unborn pup. I had lost them both during a difficult birth.

Fated mate or not, I wasn't going to find myself there again. I'd be relying on Jonas and Bryant's eventual mates to have pups to expand our family and our pack.

It wouldn't be me.

I went straight to my room to change out of my clothes. There was no meat in the fridge. We'd be hunting tonight. I wandered to the living room in the nude and waited for the other two.

*"Hurry up,"* I said through the telepathic link. *"I'm hungry."*

We would eat our fill in the forest and then haul the rest home.

Jonas: *"So impatient."*

Bryant: *"Are we looking for more venison?"*

Me: *"Whatever we can find. The cold is keeping everything in hiding."*

Jonas: *"We could haul a bear out of its den."*

Me: *"The deep freeze is on the fritz. No room for that amount of meat in the fridge."*

I could feel Jonas' disappointment through the link. It would likely be rabbits again supplemented by the meat Jonas bought in bulk through his restaurant. It was one of the reasons our family had always run a restaurant, to hide our voracious meat consumption.

Beef and bison weren't so bad when the forest wasn't offering up much. Not the same as taking down an animal, clamping tight, and feeling the warmth of its flesh as the struggle left it, the pulsing of its veins, and the warmth of its blood as it filled your mouth.

We assembled on the front porch, shifted, and took off into the forest.

Our inner wolves were set free to run and hunt.

As snow fell on my thick white fur, I had to fight the pull toward town and into the arms of my Omega—my fated mate. We needed to force him out of town—and soon.

# Chapter Three | Adam

I shivered through the sensation of the unexpected pull to shift, take off into the forest, and chase down the Alpha who was causing me to feel sick to my stomach.

It was more of an ache as if someone was reaching into my gut and clenching their hand into a fist and twisting it around. I hadn't felt it until I pressed up against Jonas in the back hall of his restaurant. It had been faint. I had thought I'd eaten too much.

I avoided eating there for the rest of the week after that.

But I was starving. I knew I couldn't stay away from the only restaurant in town and the Omega who carried the scent of my fated mate on his skin.

I gritted my teeth and pulled open the door.

It hit me like a charging bear.

The scent was coming from the back of the restaurant even though Jonas was buzzing around up front behind the counter. I nodded at him and headed for the same booth I had eaten in before. It was possible Jonas reserved it for his wolf patrons to give them a little privacy.

I regulated my breath and attempted to steady my heart rate as Jonas approached.

"What's got you all wound up?" Jonas asked.

I scowled. I had to think of something. "I have my first paying job later today."

"And that has your heart beating like a frightened rabbit?"

"I want to do a good job."

Jonas leaned his hip against the table. "How long have you been an electrician?"

"Twelve years."

"I'm sure you'll do an amazing job." Jonas touched my shoulder. The scent of his arousal was strong, but it did nothing to overpower whatever item was emitting the scent of my Alpha.

"Did you borrow someone's coat today?" I asked.

I know … it was an odd question to ask someone out of the blue, but I needed to know. Did Jonas know my fated mate? Was he close enough to him to borrow his coat?

Jonas' eyebrows rose. "My brother, Lucas's. Why?"

*Lucas.*

Just my luck. I travel hundreds of miles out into the middle of nowhere and my fated mate appears and turns out to be my rival. A pack leader, no less. I wasn't ready for that.

Fated mate or not, I was still hurting from my last relationship.

"He has a strong scent. I guess I'm missing my old pack and my pack leader."

*Lies.*

"When I heard your chosen mate abandoned you, it made me angry," Jonas said.

I nodded my head. "Thank you."

"I mean, who does that? Claims a mate and then discards them."

"An absolute bastard … trust me."

Jonas squeezed my shoulder. "I think you need some attention to forget all of that."

A shiver ran through me, and my cock pulsed. A good rut would go a long way to helping me forget. My ex-mate and the pull of this unwanted fated one.

I reached up and clung to Jonas' hip.

He interpreted my touch the way I had intended him to. He reached for me with his free hand and cradled my face, leaned down—and kissed me.

A roll of emotions surfaced.

My inner wolf growled at me. This was my fated mate's brother. A rebellious and revengeful part of me rejoiced in this. Lucas hated me and wanted to gut me.

*Payback.*

I was going to rut with his brother.

I deepened the kiss, desperate to wipe out every hunger I needed to forget—every one of them.

I inhaled to catch my breath.

*Fuck.*

The scent from the coat bore into my soul. My wolf whimpered. I couldn't do it. I pulled away from Jonas. Heading to the restroom for a quick rut felt like I'd be cheating on Lucas.

Jonas gasped; his eyes hooded with desire as he looked at me.

"Lucas," is all he said.

I nodded.

"You're his, aren't you?"

"I think so."

"Think so?" Jonas moved away from my table.

I sighed. "I know so. The draw is so strong … it's making me feel sick."

"That would explain why he's being so extra annoyed." Jonas crossed his arms and looked around. The restaurant was practically empty. Just a few humans at the far end from where I was sitting. "Then why were you considering rutting with me?"

"A bit of fun … I don't want a mate."

Jonas frowned, his brow dipped, and he moved back a step further.

"You would deny my brother his fated mate?"

The truth was: "He hasn't made a move to find me. If he wanted me, he would have tried by now." Even if he did, I wanted nothing to do with him.

"He's caught up with you being the competition."

"And I plan to continue challenging him." I matched Jonas's stance and crossed my arms. "I will undercut him by hundreds of dollars every single time."

"Oh, Omega … you do have a bit of a death wish, don't you."

"I refuse to let an Alpha push me around—fated mate or not."

"Our brother, Bryant, has been told to visit you today at your job site."

"To what?"

"Deter you and run you out of town."

"Then he better be prepared to fight me."

"He's been ordered *not* to shift."

"That's unfortunate for him then, isn't it?" I expanded my chest to increase my size. I was already intimidating but I wanted Jonas to send a message to his brother to stay away from me.

Jonas shook his head. "God … you're sexy when you're riled up."

I growled low and long.

Jonas got the message. The features of his face softened as he connected with his pack. I could follow what was likely being said based on his changing expressions. He blinked and hastily stepped back as if someone had jumped at him. He swallowed hard and chewed his bottom lip.

He exhaled and looked at me.

"Well, that was intense."

"Did you mention my connection with Lucas?"

"Oh, hell no. That's between you and him." Jonas leaned on the table with both hands. "Here's the deal. My brother, Bryant … an Alpha, by the way, will be visiting you today. Non-negotiable. Three members of the pack will be standing by in the forest nearby. If you try anything aggressive with Bryant, you will be hauled off into the forest by them and killed."

A sudden sadness washed over me. I didn't want Lucas to claim me as his, but I wanted him to long for me— miss me if I decided to leave town. Maybe even protect me ….

"That order came from Lucas? He's willing to kill his fated mate?"

"He doesn't believe you'll let it get that far?" Jonas smiled at me. "Between you and me, he's counting on it—practically praying for you to back down."

"Then why send members of his pack to threaten my life in the first place?"

"Adam, it's guttural how much he wants you gone. His wolf is pacing and snarling. The rest of the pack is confused as to why he isn't dealing with you himself."

"Then why isn't he?"

Despite my strong aversion to being in his presence, I had a deep craving to lay eyes on him. Just to see him—my fated mate. Gaze upon his features. Memorize them.

There was that fist in my gut again.

I longed for him—desperately.

"You and I both know why," Jonas said. "The pull to claim you must be strong."

I looked down at the surface of the table. "I'm not hungry

anymore." I rose from my seat, dislodging Jonas' grip on the table's edge. It was almost time for my noon appointment with the human. I'd install her lighting as promised. I had a lot to think about while I did so.

Like whether I needed to see Lucas—just once.

Plus, I had Bryant to deal with. It would be difficult not to shift—for both of us. Aggression was one of those emotions that crawled up your spine and planted the need to shift in your mind.

That and sometimes anxiety.

I was feeling a bit of both.

The human was overly hospitable, showing me where to find filtered water in the fridge to drink. She even left out a plate of home-baked cookies for me. I could tell by her demeanor and her obsession to please me that she was aware I was a wolf.

It would be different if she discovered I was an Omega. There would be no water and cookies. Just looks of disdain. I was lucky I presented as an Alpha when it came to business with humans.

Other wolves simply tolerated me.

I was in the attic wiring the recessed lighting when I caught the scent of an Alpha male. Wafting above his scent was the scent of my fated mate. They must all live together.

"Omega," a low voice boomed.

*Great.*

Now the human would know.

I climbed out of the attic covered in pink insulation and approached the Alpha. The urge to bow my head to him was strong but I resisted. He looked surprised.

And a bit impressed.

"You know why I'm here," the brother Bryant said.

"Jonas told me."

Bryant scoffed. "Of course, he did." The miffed look on his face reminded me of Jonas. But whereas Jonas was almost beautiful, Bryant was downright sexy. He was built like an American football player. Broad shoulders and chest and a broody, handsome chiseled face. You could tell they were brothers. They had the same dark hair and cocky tilt to their eyebrows.

"Do you have wolves in the forest waiting … to make sure I behave?"

"Five."

"Overkill. You must really be afraid of me."

"Lucas just wants to make sure you get the message."

"That he wants me gone? I got the message."

"If you had taken the time to introduce yourself, he might have let you join our company."

"As an employee? No thanks. I prefer to work on my own."

"That was your mistake. You should know better. Been on the side of your brothers and sisters. Instead, you're wandering around out here on your own. There would have been security for you."

I coughed out a short laugh. "By joining a pack again … never."

Bryant scowled at me. "Your mate hurt you so bad that you're willing to leave pack life?"

For a moment, I had forgotten that my life story had traveled through an entire pack—maybe two of them. Bryant knew my whole story. Or the bones of it anyway.

"Being his claimed, chosen mate wasn't good enough for him. End of story."

"Did you love him?"

I tipped my head and sighed. "Of course, I loved him."

Bryant was visibly distressed. Wolf form would have seen his hackles rising. "His actions were deplorable. Your pack leader should have come down on him."

"The pack leader is his sire."

Bryant grunted. "Shouldn't have mattered." He pressed his lips into a thin line, shut his eyes, and rolled his shoulders back. His first gaze was directly on me. "I hate to do this to you."

"Then don't."

"You know I can't disobey my Alpha leader."

"I won't go quietly. I'll shift and you'll have to haul me into the forest and try to kill me. And I know for a fact that isn't what Lucas wants."

Bryant exhaled a long breath.

"Jonas again."

"He shared his impressions of Lucas' emotions when it comes to me."

"He shouldn't have done that." Bryant walked toward me and wrapped his thick hand around my throat. His touch was light—for now. "Omega … please. Just leave town."

I windmilled my arm and knocked his hand from my throat.

I bared my emerging canines. "No!"

Bryant shoved me with both hands. "Don't make me hurt you."

I steadied my stance. "I'd like to see you try."

"Obey, Omega."

The twinge of desire to do so, to obey the Alpha, sent a shiver of anxiety through me. I inhaled a long breath. This was not the time to be having an anxiety attack.

The tingling sensation crawled from my chest to my

throat.

"Down, Omega."

My inner wolf whined and cowered. Knowing Lucas didn't want to see me dead; that he likely didn't even want me hurt … my body was not viewing Bryant as a real threat. My adrenaline was not kicking in, protecting me from the pull to obey. My ability to fight dissipated.

*God dammit.*

I sank to my knees at Bryant's feet.

"Alpha."

"Good, Omega."

If I wasn't in the Alpha's grasp, I would have cried, but only a single tear managed to escape. I slowly clenched my hands into fists. I could feel the resistance building in my mind.

*Fight.*

With every ounce of defiance I could muster, I struggled back to my feet. My muscles felt like they were on fire. I knew it was all in my mind, but it made it hard to stand with confidence.

Bryant took a step back, his eyebrows arched.

"Omega, what are you doing?"

"I told you I won't go quietly."

Bryant's eyebrows sank, coming to rest in a deep furrow. Every wrinkle on his forehead marred his attractive face. He looked conflicted.

"I'm not sure what to do with you," he said.

"You have your five wolves outside."

Bryant swayed his head to one side. "I'm not sending you out to them."

"Why not?"

"Because I'm not stupid." He stared at me. "I know why Lucas wants you gone."

"Then tell him I'm not going. I refuse to let his mating urges push me away."

"But he's your fated mate, isn't he?"

"I don't care if he is. Even if he wanted me, I'd refuse to be his."

"You have a mind of your own, Omega. Strong. You'd make a worthy mate."

The Alpha's eyes softened as he gazed at me. I sniffed the air.

*Fucking great.*

The scent of arousal was once again in the air. The Black brothers seemed to have a thing for me. Each for their own reasons. Jonas for a good time, Lucas as his fated mate—and Bryant for me being a big Omega who had unfortunately gone into his heat this morning.

"I could help you move to the next town over," Bryant said.

"And what … you'd come visit me."

Bryant took a step toward me. "Would that be so bad?"

"I'm not looking for a mate."

The Alpha growled. "And neither is Lucas."

I ran one hand through my hair. This was getting ridiculous. I just wanted to be left alone. No one-night stands. No fated mate. No being a kept wolf in the next town.

There was only one thing to do.

I needed to confront Lucas.

# Chapter Four | Lucas

The message coming through from Bryant was not what I wanted to hear. He had failed miserably in what I had asked him to do. The Omega had gotten under his skin.

Now Adam was headed here to the house.

I thought about hopping into my truck and taking off for a drive but before I could, Bryant gunned it up the driveway, and slid to a stop behind my vehicle, blocking me in.

He came running into the house, charging at me.

"Mine, Alpha … he's mine!"

"You can't have him, Bryant."

"You don't even want him!" My brother's stance was something I wasn't used to seeing. He was in full-on protective mode.

I growled and shoved Bryant. "Back down, brother."

"You won't see or sense him. I'll keep him in Riverton."

My chest swelled, creaking, and I could feel bones shifting along my spine. My canines lengthened, pressing into my bottom lip. My vision focused itself solely on Bryant.

I was mere moments away from shifting.

"You will keep him *nowhere*!" I roared.

"He's mine!" Bryant surged at me, snarling.

The sound of tires crunching gravel made us both turn. The scent of my fated Omega filled my senses. It was the closest he had ever been to me. Fighting his appeal at a distance had been difficult enough—but this. My inner wolf howled at length. *"Mine! All mine!"*

Through our glass front door, I could see my Omega collapse on the stairs outside. He appeared to be in pain. His face screwed up in distress, he reached for the next step with one hand.

He was fighting his progress up the steps, I could tell.

Bryant and I made a run for the door. He hauled it open before I had a chance. He dashed to my Omega's side and put an arm around him.

He was touching *my* Omega.

Heat—rage.

*Mine!*

I launched myself at Bryant. My chest hit his shoulder and knocked him over, tumbling down the stairs. We shook and groaned as we started our shift. I was full wolf moments before him. I took advantage and found an unprotected piece of furless flesh on his thigh.

I latched on and tore.

Bryant screamed. Then fur filled my mouth. But he was already injured. He stumbled away from me and circled my position. I wasn't going to wait for him to come at me.

The Omega was mine.

I charged at him, and we collided in a frenzy of flying fur, hard muscular bodies, and sharp gnashing teeth. I asserted my dominance, backing him up and growling. When I achieved a good purchase on his limbs or muzzle, Bryant would yip, but he wouldn't back down.

We tumbled, bashing into the posts of the deck. Panting, paws flying, my jaws trying to achieve a firm hold on his throat that would signify the intent of bringing about his death.

He escaped and stumbled away from me.

Bryant's left rear leg was coated in blood. He limped toward me, his head hanging low. I could see the pain in his eyes. He looked over his shoulder, then turned and ran in that direction.

My attention was immediately on Adam.

He was panting and quivering on the stairs. Jonas was at his side, attempting to calm him. To offer him the support of another Omega during such a critical moment.

I shifted to non-wolf, shivering in the cold air against bare skin, and approached Adam. I took my time. I didn't want to frighten him. I didn't know for certain how he was going to react to me.

I just knew I needed him.

I leaned toward him, nuzzled his hair with my cheek, and rubbed my shoulder against his. I whined as I backed away to give him space. I desperately wanted to press my body against his.

He looked up at me, his eyes like soft brown saucers filled with tears, his mouth open, whimpering. It was an invitation to approach his side again. When I was close enough, he clung to my thigh, then my arm, then my face. He fixed his gaze on mine, whining.

I joined him in the sound of desperation. Both of his hands cradled my face. He touched my nose with his, then my Omega brought our lips together—and the entire universe fell into place.

*Mine.*

The slap across my face the next moment was unexpected.

"Asshole!" Adam shouted.

Then he sank back onto my lips, hand clutching my face. His kiss was frenzied. A mixture of desire and furious annoyance. I wasn't sure if he wanted to mate with me or kill me.

I chanced my life on the first.

I pulled our lips apart and touched my forehead to his so we could continue sharing breath. I held his face and stroked my thumb along his cheekbone. The scent of his heat was overpowering. I wanted to plunge deep inside him—to fill him with my seed.

"You're mine," I whispered.

Adam gripped my arm and dug his fingernails in until I was certain he had drawn blood. He was struggling with this part of our union.

"And you're mine," he said at last.

I sealed those bonding words with a kiss. He melted against me, the fight draining out of him. My Omega was strong. He had resisted saying those words longer than I thought possible.

He relaxed, supple, and curled up against my chest, his hand on my collarbone as I lifted him into my arms. He kissed my jaw as I carried him into the forest.

The cabin, the original homestead on the property, was nearly twenty minutes into the trees very near a branch of the creek. I kept it clean and stocked for those days when I needed to get away from my brothers and have time alone. And to immerse myself in memories of my mate.

Now, I was doing something I never thought I'd do by bringing a new mate to the cabin. A fated mate. One I'd had no chance of avoiding. I kissed Adam's forehead, and he smiled up at me.

The last few steps, he hummed against my throat.

Content, I lay him on the bedding and fussed about starting a fire. My skin felt like ice. As an Alpha, I ran extremely hot, but walking through a cold, breezy forest naked in my bare feet had only been made tolerable because Adam's warm, clothed body had been against my chest.

The fire roaring, I approached the bed.

Adam had stripped out of his coat and boots and had one side of the comforter wrapped over his shoulders. He watched me with a careful gaze. There was still a little fight left in him.

We would go at his pace.

"Can I kiss you again?" I asked him.

Adam flung the comforter aside and reached for me.

*That would be a yes.*

I crawled across the bed toward him. There was such desire in his eyes, his pupils blown, watching me; his eyelashes fluttering—gasping lips parted.

Waiting for me.

He was perfection.

I layered my body on him as he guided me to him. His muscular arms wrapped around my chest once I settled my weight on him. I had no concerns about crushing him. Our bodies existed in nearly equal tandem. He was slightly shorter than me—his toes only reaching my ankles.

Adam tipped his head and captured my mouth, then licked my bottom lip, and chased it with his teeth. He was a bit of a tease. I liked that.

I met his tongue with mine and we danced outside our mouths, licking and tasting, before joining our lips. Again, the stars aligned. He was my fated mate and I wanted all of him.

I ground my hips against him, my cock thickening, and he flung his legs around my thighs, pinning me tighter to him. He undulated up into each one of my thrusts.

The clothes on his body became maddening.

I grabbed the bottom of his shirt and pulled it off over his head. He smiled up at me once the shirt was clear of his face. So innocent—so pure. Even though I knew he wasn't.

I dove back into him, seeking to claim him using my mouth on his alone. Each meeting brought a torrent of emotions so primal that I gave up trying to make sense of them.

He was mine—that's all I knew.

And I was his—forever his.

And we needed to mate. To bond our connection.

Adam lowered his arms and reached between us, He fought with his button and fly until they relented, then I helped him squirm out of his pants and underwear.

The first feel of his naked body beneath me was like seeing a full moon for the first time. It was so glorious as to be without words to describe it.

I kissed his lips, then his jaw, then his throat. I dragged my lips along his collarbone until I reached the area behind his ear where his scent was strongest.

I inhaled deeply.

There was no mistaking we were fated.

Adam nuzzled my ear, humming, and then licked my neck near my shoulder where he might claim me someday. I groaned as he sucked on the ceremonial flesh.

"My mate," he whispered.

Those words were a step short of him biting into me, sucking on my blood, and claiming me as his forever. The day would come. We needed time together first.

I shifted downward and kissed his sternum. Adam lifted his arms over his head and draped them across his dark hair. If he was a cat, he would have been purring.

Instead, his wolf growled softly.

At peace.

I kissed a line down between his ribs until I reached his belly. It was ridged and hard. I licked a swath with the flat of my tongue between each section of muscle. He tasted salty and musky.

He was pure wolf.

The top of his hard cock grazed my chin. I sat back and looked down into his eyes. I wouldn't touch his cock for the first time without his permission.

Adam reached for my thigh and caressed it.

"I'm *all* yours, Alpha … *all* yours."

I lowered my chest and kissed each of his hip bones. He squirmed beneath my lips, pushing his cock toward me. That made me smile. My Omega had no trouble asking for what he wanted. He would present me with a challenge at times—a challenge I was willing to take on.

I hummed as I ran my lips along his shaft. He jammed his hand into my hair and held me from retreating. I used one hand to steady his cock as I licked the head. I sucked on the slit, coating my lips in pre-cum. He was hungry for me. I encased his cockhead with my mouth and eased him across my tongue to the back of my throat. I sucked hard, bobbing up and down, as I toyed with his shaft with the flat of my tongue. I retreated, spat on his cock, and caressed it in my palm.

Adam's hands went into his hair.

"Fuck," he whispered as he watched me.

I lifted one ball and then the other into my mouth, sucking and wetting them. They were pink and full amongst the abundance of thick hair between his thighs.

Adam raised his knees into his hands, feet dangling near my shoulders. I used my thumbs to part the hair near his hole and slid one thumb inside. He was slick and ready.

The warmth of his body amplified the scent coming from him.

He was in full heat.

I looked up at his beautiful, expectant face. I must have

looked concerned.

"I'm on birth control," he whispered to me.

It was the answer I needed. I brought my knees up under his ass, leaned forward, and kissed him. This kiss was different. It was a pact between us. What happened in the next few moments was important. This wasn't simply rutting. This was a joining of two fated mates.

Adam tipped his head back and sighed as I pressed my cockhead past his tight ring. I dug my knees into the bedding, angled my hips, and sank into him. He clung to my shoulders and whimpered as I closed in against his ass. My perfect mate had taken me inside in one go.

"My mate," I whispered.

"Mine," Adam responded.

I steadied the position of my hands to either side of his shoulders. As I rocked back and forth into him, our lips took their time to become acquainted for a lifetime together.

Adam growled, pulled away, and looked up at me. There was animalistic desire burning in his eyes. He growled again; his lips parted. His canines were fully descended.

My body reacted. My gums pulsed as my canines lengthened in my mouth. I headed back to that spot behind Adam's ear. I inhaled and dragged my canines along his neck. I teased the claiming area of his shoulder with my lips and teeth. I did my best to suck on the area.

Adam became frantic beneath me. Legs wrapped around my hips, trapping me. Lifting his ass to meet my thrusts. Fingers clawing my shoulders. Panting—chest heaving.

It started low in Adam's chest. The soft howl—then louder.

The response filled my gut. I met his howl with one of my own. Our mating song was transcendent. Perfect unison.

Meant to be. Fated mates.

I thrust hard into him as a knot swelled at the base of my cock. It would trap me inside of him until it either subsided or he was experienced enough to milk my seed from me.

Adam pulled me to his chest and clung to me.

"Fill me, Alpha." He stirred, adjusting his position, pressed his heels into the bedding, and lifted his hips. I closed my eyes and gasped as the length of his hole clenched down hard on the entirety of my cock. He lowered his hips and clenched again, this time sighing and groaning.

The result was a rolling ripple of pressure from the base of my cock to the tip—again and again. The effect was an escalation of undulating sensation. He rocked his hips with each inner caress, starting slow and then increasing in pace with my response to him.

I lowered my mouth to his shoulder. The need to claim him was incredible. He was driving me into a state of wildness I could barely contain. I panted fast and hard against his skin.

"I'm yours," Adam called to me as he dug his hand into my hair. I wasn't sure if he was giving me permission to claim him so early in our relationship. Even if he was, I was going to wait.

"And I'm yours, my mate," I replied.

A soul-extracting ripple cascaded up the length of my cock. I growled and fought the urge to bite Adam as my knot released and I flooded my mate with seed.

Adam growled and rolled me onto my back, still seated on my cock.

He began stroking his own.

"I hate you, you know?" Adam said.

"Why?"

"I believe there was talk of you gutting me."

"That's before I met you."

"You *just* met me."

"And now, I would never let anyone hurt you."

"Even you?"

I gripped his thighs. I knew Adam's history. There was no reason he should trust me. Except he wasn't chosen—he was my fated mate. I'd crawl into the bush and die before I ever let anyone cause him pain—including myself. I took over stroking his cock.

"You're my fated mate," I said. "I take that very seriously."

Adam watched me while inhaling deeply.

I was speaking the truth.

He smacked my hand away, lifted himself off my softening cock, and took his shaft back into his own palm. He put his other hand on my chest. "You're going to lie there."

I would've growled and tossed him off me if his commanding voice hadn't been so sexy. He was going to be trouble. An Omega with the inklings of an Alpha mind would keep me busy.

Adam pumped his cock faster as he bit his bottom lip. He tossed his head back, swearing and growling. My cock thickened at the sight of him towering above me.

His other hand held me in place.

I squeezed his thighs as his hips bucked and he shot spurts of seed onto my chest and belly. He rode the waves of his release with soft mewling noises. So sweet, I wanted to mate with him all over again. But we had things to talk about first. We barely knew each other.

Adam landed on the bedding beside me. He turned onto his side and traced circles on my shoulder with his pointer finger. He leaned forward and kissed where he'd drawn the last circle.

"What were you like as a young pup?" Adam asked.

"Rambunctious and serious all at the same time. It was clear early on I was going to be pack leader someday. I was always keeping my brothers and other pups in line."

Adam snorted. "So, you were a bully."

I turned on my side to face him. "I never said that. I was very nice about it."

"Even when you're planning to gut fated mates?"

"You need to drop that." I stroked the back of my fingers along his arm from his shoulder down to his elbow. "I never would have hurt you. I just needed you to leave."

"Why? Why was it so important to run me out of town?"

"I could sense you."

"I could sense you too, but I had no intention of running away."

I looked into his expressive, soft brown eyes as I smiled at him and brushed a strand of dark hair from his forehead. "So … what was your long-term plan to stay away from me?"

Adam lowered his gaze, so he wasn't looking at me. "I didn't have one."

"We would have encountered each other eventually."

"And I would have found myself falling to the ground and crawling toward you."

"That upsets you, doesn't it?"

He nodded. "That I couldn't resist you … of course, it does."

"Are you still upset?"

Adam caught my gaze again. "You're my fated mate … my Alpha. Mating with you helped strip some of that fury away, but we have a long path ahead of us." He touched my lower lip and chased my mouth for a kiss, then tipped his head away. "And I'm willing to walk it with you."

I pulled Adam closer to me. "Tell me about your puphood. Did you grow up in the city?"

"I did. Small family. Just my sire and my carrier and me."

"Both males?"

"No, my carrier was an Alpha female."

"Both were Alphas?"

I could feel Adam's smile against my cheek. "Yup."

"That would explain a lot about your size and disposition."

He lifted his head and looked at me with one eyebrow cocked. "What's wrong with my disposition?"

I laughed. He was teasing me. "You're a handful, that's all."

Adam placed his hand on my stomach after it grumbled.

"Should we hunt?" he asked.

Our first hunt together. It was another milestone. Until we claimed each other, we wouldn't be able to hear one another in our minds. Hunting without the connection would be difficult. We would need to rely on watching each other's body language.

It would be a true test of our compatibility.

"We can head north," I replied. "A couple of hours from the house. There is often game roaming at this time of year. Deer. Maybe some boar."

"Then let's hunt. It's been over a week since I tasted fresh meat. Longer since I hunted any. Living in the city meant we had to travel by car to wooded areas. It wasn't ideal."

"You're going to love living here with the forest right outside your door."

Adam gave me a subtle scowl.

"I'm not ready for that yet," he said. "Living with you. I

like my little suite."

I nodded. He was right. Now that we had mated, we could take things slow. Get to know each other. Spend some time enjoying each other without complicating things. Bryant would probably crawl back to the house eventually. I wasn't sure how he'd react to Adam's presence in the house.

"I'll let you set the pace," I said.

"Thank you."

Adam rolled away from me and rose from the bed. The firelight danced on his skin, creating shadows in some areas, and bright spots in others. My heart ached for him. I wanted him to come back to bed so I could mate with him again. Then burrow into the blankets together.

Adam growled.

I joined him, our throats vibrating in unison, as I climbed off the bed.

The promise of the pulsing thrill latched onto my thoughts.

My wolf saw red.

Adam led the way outside. I waited and watched as he shifted into the most glorious black wolf I had ever set eyes on. He wandered over to me and touched my hand with his wet nose.

He whined as I ran my fingers through the thick fur on his head.

He was anxious to get going.

I stepped away and shifted. As I caught my breath, my wolf senses came alive. I rubbed my head against Adam's. Against his ear. Against his jaw. The top of his muzzle.

He joined in until we were shoving each other playfully. Adam pounded his two paws into the ground in unison shoulder-width apart, dipping forward. His eyes were wild—

his tongue out.

An invitation to frolic.

I would have laughed if I could.

Adam took off into the trees at top speed and I followed him. I caught up with him a few times and tried to pounce on him, but he was fast and scooted out from under me.

After a while, we slowed to a steady pace. We needed to conserve our energy. I took the lead and Adam stayed close behind. He didn't know these woods like I did.

We headed north. Two hours away from the house, we finally caught sight of some boar. A dangerous adversary with only two of us.

I needn't have worried. Adam was skilled and large enough that I felt as if I was hunting with another Alpha. We soon had a beast on the ground, writhing and squealing.

Adam finished it off.

I tore into its belly first where it was warm and soft—the best bits. Adam stood back, watching me. For the first time in my life, it felt uncomfortable having an Omega wait his turn.

I stopped; my muzzle bloody and dripping, and turned to him.

He backed away a couple of steps. I was confusing him by hesitating.

I shook my head to disperse some of the blood from my fur and walked away from the kill. Adam took a tentative step forward. Then another. I waited on the outskirts of our killing area.

Adam dipped his head as he looked at me, sniffing the air.

He took another step toward the boar.

He sniffed the ground and then the torn edge of the belly. He licked a small section and then checked over his shoulder to where I was standing.

There was a slight wag of his tail as he crouched down and took his first real bite of the delicate innards. Being an Omega, he'd likely never enjoyed the delicacy. I wanted to give him the world. He would be my partner in every sense. In and out of wolf form.

Once Adam ate his fill, he backed away and bowed to me. I rushed the carcass and began working on the ribs. Adam crouched on the ground and used his paws to clean some of the blood from his muzzle, wiping his fur with his forearms and licking them.

Not satisfied, he shifted back to non-wolf form.

"I smell water. Is it close?"

I turned my head toward the stream and took off in the direction of it. Adam shifted back and followed. He had to run to catch up. That had taken a lot of strength, shifting back-to-back like that. The pain must have been incredible. My mate was beautiful, powerful, and tough.

It made me proud of him.

Proud to call him my mate.

He caught up and shifted back to non-wolf once we were at the stream's edge. He waded into the frigid water. His body was still running hot from being in wolf form. He scrubbed his face and arms, dispensing with the blood. I decided to shift to non-wolf form and join him.

Before I had a chance to clean myself, Adam had me in his arms, kissing me, smearing blood back over his face near his mouth. He'd need to bathe again.

He whimpered against my lips, slipped from my arms, and dropped to hands and knees at the edge of the stream, his hands on land, his knees in the water.

I knelt beside him and placed my hands in the mud.

I nudged his face with mine and bit his bottom lip. I

whined as I pressed our bodies together, shoulder to shoulder. I rubbed against him, straightened, and slung my arms to either side of his back. I followed his scent from the back of his neck, down his spine to the pungent scent of his heat. I kneeled behind him. His hole was wet. I dove for it, running my tongue through the musky fluid. The growl Adam emitted traveled through his body to my deeply buried face.

I clamped my hands on his ass cheeks and pried him open further. I licked and prodded until Adam was close to howling. Moments before he did, I plunged my cock inside him.

A haunting song of howling pleasure and contentment floated across the air. I had a few hiccups of a howl, and then it burst free, mixing with Adam's.

No one in the vicinity would mistake our pure, harmonized chorus for anything other than the joining of fated mates. It was a message. The leader of the East Creekside pack had found his one and only; the male he would spend the rest of his life with. Our union meant I would be perceived as stronger. I had a formidable Omega at my side. We'd be unstoppable.

I grunted as I filled my mate. I clutched his hips and pumped into him until I was spent. I pulled away. As an Alpha, even with a fated mate, I had no obligation to make sure my mate reached climax. It was different with Adam, though. I already cherished him.

I would deny him nothing.

I turned Adam onto his back and positioned myself between his legs, my chest on the bed of the stream, my legs in the water. The cold water served to calm my cock.

Adam stroked my head as I sucked him until he filled my throat with his exquisite seed. I cleaned his cockhead with my tongue, languishing until we both started shivering.

Adam smiled at me. "How are we going to get that carcass to the cabin? I'm freezing."

"There are wolves in the area."

Adam sniffed the air. "They're miles away."

"They'll find it."

"It's your pack. I won't argue with you."

"It's your pack now too."

Adam scowled. "Forgot about that part."

"You're that set against having a pack."

"It's a lot of noise."

I pulled myself up the bank and sat beside Adam. I wrapped my arm around his shoulders and pulled him to me. He rested his head against mine.

"If it's important, the speaker will holler. Don't listen otherwise."

"I feel compelled to, but it messes with my head."

"Why?"

Adam gripped my arm. "I have a problem with anxiety. Like an actual disorder."

"That's unusual." I kissed his head. "Did your sire or carrier have anxiety?"

"Not that they were willing to speak about."

"What can I do to help?"

"Give me time to adjust. Support me."

"I can do that. I'm yours now. I promise we'll tackle it together."

"Can we go back to the cabin now?" Adam pulled away. Apparently, we were finished with that conversation. Maybe he'd tell me more later.

I looked at his face. Around his mouth was covered in blood. I could heat some water for us to bathe properly back at the cabin. There was a metal bathtub we'd both fit in.

"I'm going to spoil you and wash you when we get back," I said. "A long hot bath."

Adam hummed and smiled. "I love that idea."

I struggled to my feet and shifted. I shook out my fur. I was at the limit of shifts for one day. My body was aching something fierce. Once more back to non-wolf and then I planned to keep Adam in that bed for days, mating with him until he was loose and open and filled with my seed.

# Chapter Five | Adam

The next ten days after our first mating were glorious. We had holed up in the cabin, fully immersed in each other. Jonas had been bringing us meat so we could spend our time getting to know one another. Talking and mating. Mating and talking. In continuous rotation with short breaks to eat and sleep. I wouldn't be surprised if we could map out each other bodies by now.

I had explored every inch of Lucas' muscular flesh, nibbling, sucking—tasting. He was pure Alpha, and I couldn't get enough of him. My body was no longer responding on a genetic level. We'd moved past that. I was drawn to him now because he was my mate.

And he was incredible.

Hours of talking had dispelled my preconceived notions about him. He was a commanding but even-tempered leader; I could tell by the way he carried himself when he spoke to Jonas. In private when it was just us, he softened, treating me with incredible affection and devotion.

Listening to the stories of his life, I discovered he was gentle and giving and valued integrity in everything he did. He was an honorable and hard-working wolf. Pack and family were the most important aspects of life to him, and he found joy in the smallest things.

And his sense of humor … it was dry and left me in fits of laughter and tears.

Plus, he was gorgeous to look at. Dark hair, piercing grey eyes, and flushed pink lips made for kissing. He had both the beauty of Jonas and the sexiness of Bryant.

My heart skipped a beat each time I took a moment to study him.

His smile—sublime.

So earnest and soul-melting.

And Lucas was an incredible lover, taking his time with my body before mating with me.

I cuddled against Lucas' side. I'd lost count of how many times we'd mated. My hole was relaxed and no longer objected, and my balls and inner thighs were coated in dried seed.

I'd never been happier.

It was undeniable.

I was falling for him.

"What are you thinking about?" Lucas asked.

I smiled at him. "You … and how I don't hate you anymore."

Lucas laughed. "I'm pleased to hear that … I no longer want to gut you."

I gripped his chin and kissed him. I lingered and then set my gaze on his.

"We need to go back to work," I said. "Both of us."

Lucas groaned and rolled his eyes. "I knew this wouldn't last forever."

"Did you want it to?"

Lucas growled and wrapped his hand around the back of my neck. "I never want to stop mating with you and hearing tales of your life. Whispering secrets and exploring your mind. Our time together here has been precious. I can't wait for us to start our life together."

I touched his face. "Just give me some time. Get all of this straight in my head."

"I'll be waiting, mate. Waiting to welcome you into *our*

home."

The way he said *our* brought tears to my eyes. This was my fated mate. I'd found him. That couldn't be said of everyone. Many wolves went without ever finding their mate.

I was incredibly lucky.

And grateful.

I just needed a minute to prepare myself for the next part of our union. I didn't want to rush it. I wanted to be sure there was more than DNA bringing us together. I ached for those three words to be spoken. By both of us. I wanted us to have connected on a spiritual level.

"I won't be long," I said.

Lucas kissed me, slow and with so many messages. He longed for me the way I longed for him. We had become more than an Alpha and his Omega. He wanted to share his life with me.

Not command me.

Instinctively, I knew we were destined to become equals. I could feel it. We would take our rightful places in the hierarchy of the pack as strong partners.

I stayed near his mouth and kissed his chin.

Once again without pups, though.

Lucas had told me what happened to his mate and their unborn pup. How pupbirth had taken them both. Lucas had loved his chosen mate and was terrified to try again to produce offspring—to bolster the pack size. It was an unpopular decision amongst the pack, but Lucas was firm in it.

I would stay on birth control.

There would be no pups.

I needed him to mate with me one more time before I left. I stroked my hand up his thigh and sought out his cock from between us. It was flaccid but hardened in my hand.

I sighed as he rolled me onto my back and filled me again. Even the rhythm of our hearts matched. We moved against each other in a synchronized dance we had now performed many times. It was perfection. Our bodies fit together like molecules of water. We were one.

As we lay curled up in the comforter, satisfied, Lucas gazed at me with sadness in his eyes.

"I'm going to close my eyes," he said. "So, I don't see you leave."

I licked my lips. This was going to be heart-wrenching. "Okay."

He closed his eyes and I rose from the bed. My clothes were abandoned where I had tossed them over a week ago. I pulled them on. They felt strange against my skin. I could live quite happily every day in wolf form and naked every night in non-wolf form with Lucas.

But that wasn't the world we lived in.

I had to head back to work. There were hopefully emails piled up, waiting for me to go out and give quotes. Lucas and I hadn't talked much about my business other than I should continue doing the small jobs for now. Lucas was going to pull Bryant off them … if he ever came back.

Jonas had reported he hadn't seen or sensed Bryant anywhere near the house or in town. His absence was concerning Lucas. It wasn't in Bryant's nature to become a lone wolf.

I finished dressing and quietly slipped out the door. I followed the scent of woodsmoke until I arrived back at Lucas' house where my truck was parked. I stood back and looked up at the massive structure. All hand-hewn logs. Likely assembled over 100 years ago by Lucas' ancestors. Two stories with a new, green metal roof and a wide porch that ran the full perimeter.

This would someday be my home.

I glanced over from the house Lucas shared with his brothers—now only Jonas. There were two more log homes in the clearing—smaller ones. The entirety of the pack. It was possible there were less than ten wolves altogether in Lucas' East Creekside pack.

One of those homes contained Lucas' sister, Carina. He'd told me all about her. About how challenging it had been growing up with an Alpha female. Some of the stories reminded me of my Alpha carrier. *Mom* as the humans would call her. She had been devastated when I told her I was moving away. What would she think now? When I told her I'd found my fated mate.

Jonas wandered out onto the front porch.

"Everything go well?" he asked.

I smirked. "My ass is sore."

Jonas laughed. "Good sign, but what about connecting?" I must have looked wistful because Jonas smiled at me. "That good, hey," he said.

"Incredible."

"I knew you two would get along eventually."

I clung to the banister and put my foot on the bottom step. The same steps I had fought to stop myself from climbing; the pull toward my fated mate causing me pain as I struggled against it.

"It's more than *getting along*," I said. "I'm feeling something."

"So soon?" Jonas took a few steps down toward me. "Did you claim each other?"

I shook my head. "Not yet. I'm waiting … waiting for those three words to flow between us. We're headed that way, though. My inner wolf can feel it deep in my heart."

Jonas rubbed his lips as his eyes filled with tears. He shook his hands as if to dispel the emotions and jogged down the rest of the steps to me. He threw his arms around me and hugged me so tight, I thought he might squeeze the breath out of me. I hugged him back.

Jonas was my brother now.

"It'll happen," he whispered against my ear. "I know it will. I can sense it."

We pulled back from the hug and lingered for a moment as if there might be more to say. I was honestly out of things to say. I just wanted to go back to my little room and process.

"I'm gonna go," I said at last.

"Yeah, you probably need to rest."

"That and Lucas will be back here soon. We don't need to suffer through another farewell. Leaving his side was brutal." I touched my chest. "My heart is hurting."

Jonas clasped his hands together. "I'm so happy for you both."

"Thanks." I offered him a weak smile, turned from him, and climbed into my truck. I was exhausted. I barely registered the drive back to the boarding house other than the pull to Lucas softened a little. It was a good place for him to be—waiting in the back of my mind.

I flopped down on my bed and kicked off my boots. They thumped onto the floor. I tugged a pillow under my head and descended into a deep sleep.

I SAT UP SLOWLY in bed. I wasn't sure if I was hungry or sleep deprived. The room didn't feel right. I sniffed the air. It smelled like broccoli. There were two humans in the boarding house, so vegetables were a necessary part of the daily meals.

My stomach rolled at the stench.

I checked the clock. It was dinner time. I'd slept through most of the day. The room was pitch black. In non-wolf form, I needed lights at night. I leaned over and flicked on the light beside my bed. It seemed brighter than normal. I almost switched it off again.

I rose to my feet and had to catch myself on the bedside table. The room had swayed a little. I smirked. Lucas had mated me into a state of delirium. It was going to take a while to recover.

I jogged down the steps and into the dining room.

Mama offered me a warm smile. Of course, by now, she would know that Lucas and I had found each other. That we had spent 10 days mating.

"It's nice to see you back, Adam," one of the humans said. A kindly older gentleman. "Did you have business out of town?"

I grinned. "Something like that."

He nodded at me. "I trust the conclusion was satisfactory."

"Oh, yes … very."

I looked at Mama. Her cheeks were rosy with the ferocity of her smile. This was big news, their pack leader finding his fated mate. The pack would be in a better position because of it.

The West Creekside's pack leader was unmated.

Mama returned to the kitchen and reemerged with two dishes to add to the roasted chickens on the table. Potatoes and the dreaded broccoli.

The smell of the latter wafted over me.

I slapped my hand over my mouth and nose.

*Fuck.*

It smelled worse than usual. My stomach flipped, nausea rose from my chest to my temples and made the glands in my throat pinch. The wooden panels of the walls appeared to ripple.

I'd never reacted that violently before.

Mama was peering at me with part concern—part expectation.

I leaped up from the table. "Excuse me," I muttered then made my way to the restroom on the main floor to splash some cold water on my face.

Instead, I found myself on my knees in front of the toilet. I poised my face above the porcelain bowl and threw up. The nausea didn't relent. It came back around and had me dry retching.

A soft knock on the door. "Adam, do you need anything?"

*Mama.*

"No, I'm fine."

I spent a moment going through what I had eaten over the past day. It had all been fresh meat. This wasn't food poisoning. I gripped the toilet bowl seat with both hands.

It wasn't possible.

Was it?

The toilet bowl swam in front of my eyes. Sweating, I heaved out a cough and some bile. Absolutely not food poisoning. I placed my forehead on the cold porcelain.

*Oh, for fuck's sake.*

I was about to ask Mama for a two-month ginger supply to hold me until the end of gestation when she hammered on the door, frantic.

"West Creekside, Adam!"

I stumbled to my feet and hauled open the door. I had suspected this might happen. So had Lucas. Bryant wasn't coming back, but he wasn't going to go quietly.

"They crossed the creek," I stated flatly.

"Bryant has teamed up with their pack. They've surrounded our houses." She gripped my arms. "Oh, Adam … this is bad. They outnumber us." Lucas had failed to mention that to me. We hadn't talked about the West Creekside pack other than the possibility they might take Bryant in.

I'd never been in a fight for territory before. I had been too young the last time my pack had boundary issues. Lucas' pack was my pack now. I'd fight alongside him as his mate.

"I need to get back to the house," I said as I pushed Mama aside.

She gripped my arm tightly. "Oh, no, you don't."

I yanked on my arm, but she refused to let go. "Mama, I have to go be with Lucas. I need to help protect our pack and our home. Numbers matter."

"Not when you're carrying our leader's pup, they don't."

"I'm just a little sick to my stomach. Bad meat."

"After ten full days of mating … I don't believe that for a second."

Mama was right. Being at the height of my heat meant my birth control was more likely to fail. Statistically with the number of times we had mated, a pup was the reason for my nausea.

"Mama … please. Lucas needs me." I didn't want to continue arguing with her. I needed to get to Lucas. I was less than a week pregnant. I was willing to risk it and fight.

*Lucas.*

I slumped against the door frame. Lucas wouldn't be willing to risk it. His fated mate was carrying his pup. I placed my hand on my belly. I was carrying *our* pup.

"Okay," I said, and Mama released my arm. Two fat tears

rolled down my cheeks. The first opportunity to support my new pack and I had to let them down. I imagined Lucas and Jonas out there in wolf form, fighting other wolves … fighting their brother.

Blood and fur flying.

I might not ever see either one of them again. A rush of anxiety rose into my throat and spread to my fingertips. I needed to get control of myself. I inhaled and exhaled a long breath.

I met her concerned gaze. "You've told Lucas about the pup already, haven't you?"

Mama nodded. "I had to. It'll give him something more to fight for."

"He doesn't even want pups."

Mama patted my shoulder. "He'll want this one." She gave me a little shove. "Now, go and lie down. I'll get you some fresh ginger tea and make sure you have everything you need."

As I lay in bed, I couldn't help but dissect Mama's words. She had said, "He'll want this one," when referring to her conversation with Lucas, not, "He *wants* this one."

# Chapter Six | Lucas

I couldn't let it break my focus; the reason Adam couldn't fight at my side. Without my Omega, my position in the pack during a dispute could be challenged. Typically, wolves carrying pups weren't exempt from supporting the pack against threats.

This was different.

I wanted to place Adam on a cloud, safe high above the ground. Protected from the world.

Him and our pup.

I gripped the banister along the frontside of our deck as a repeating terror from my past rolled through me. I was going to lose them. It would happen again.

The thought wouldn't leave my mind.

Jonas rested his hand on my shoulder. "Don't think that. Your Omega is strong. In two months, you'll have a chubby, furry pup fast asleep on your chest after a big feed."

"I want to believe that."

"Then do." Jonas looked across the clearing in front of our house into the forest. "How many of them do you think are out there?"

"At least fifteen."

"It feels weird not having Bryant with us."

I searched my mind, checking every telepathic connection I'd once had with my brother. I couldn't find him. "He's masked himself somehow."

"Alpha," Jonas whispered. "Is it possible Bryant was claimed by one of them?"

The thought had crossed my mind. Joining another pack

by having one of its members claim him seemed a bit extreme. But it was Bryant. He was an Alpha with an uneven temperament. That's why even though Bryant was older than me, he hadn't been chosen to be the leader of our pack.

Now he was gone.

All because of Adam—my fated Omega.

"It's possible," I responded.

Bryant should never have expected me to give Adam up to him. Let him keep him in the next township over. The plan had been to run Adam out of town because he was mine.

Not make him up for grabs.

Not have Bryant take him as his chosen mate.

Adam would never have gone with Bryant anyway. We were fated. No matter what I did to try and get rid of him, he would've felt the pull to stay. It may well be what led him to Creekside.

An ancient, inner spiritual wolf whispering in his ear.

Something had brought us together across the miles.

Now, he was carrying our pup.

"That's how fate works, Alpha," Jonas said. "When it's working properly." He picked at the flaking paint on the banister. "Not that I would know anything about that."

I wrapped my arm around Jonas' shoulders. "You'll find him, Omega. Your Alpha."

Jonas sighed. "Do you think they're waiting for sunrise?"

I shifted into telepathic mode to the entire pack. Jonas was proving himself to be a good second in command now that Bryant was gone. *"We think they might be waiting for first light."*

*"We'll be ready."* A resounding response from all nine wolves in the next houses.

*"Lucas!"*

It was Mama.

Mama: *"I'm sorry, Alpha ... he's gone. Adam. He's not in his room."*

Me: *"Did you check the house?"*

Mama: *"His truck is gone. It's not parked anywhere on the street."*

My heart thudded hard in my chest and felt like it dropped into my belly. I was overtaken by absolute panic. I inhaled, searching for my Omega—I couldn't detect him.

Me: *"Are his belongings still there?"*

Mama: *"Oh, Alpha ... I'm so sorry. I don't know why he ran."*

I looked out at the forest. I couldn't leave and look for Adam. Not now. My pack needed to come first. No matter how much I wanted to run, I had ten wolves relying on me.

When Mama had told me about the pup, I had been conflicted. Adam would have been waiting for some kind of reassurance from me that I wanted this pup. The last we had spoken, I had told him, I didn't want to attempt to bring any pups into the world. That it was too risky.

I may have been very firm in my language regarding it.

He may have jumped to conclusions.

"Maybe he headed back to his pack," Jonas said.

I shook my head. "He wouldn't do that."

"He's a pregnant male Omega. They'd protect him. He needs a chaperone."

"He's also stubborn." If anything, he'd taken off to raise the pup somewhere on his own. Somewhere his fated mate's insecurities wouldn't interfere.

I glowered into the darkness.

I'd done this.

I'd chased my true fate mate away.

*Adam.*

I shoved myself away from the banister and growled low in my throat. My latest inhalation had been filled with the scent of my Omega. What was he doing *here*?

My emotions alternated between aggravated panic and heart-flooding relief.

He hadn't run away … he'd run home.

I charged down to the parking area. Sure enough, his truck was coming up the long driveway, lights bobbing with each pothole. I was fuming by the time he climbed out of his vehicle.

"What the hell are you doing here!" I rushed at him.

Adam slammed his truck door closed and took a defensive stance.

"Protecting my family."

"That's why you were supposed to stay at Mama's. To protect our family."

"I'm no use there. I refuse to be locked up and pampered when I have the strength of an Alpha to contribute to defending our home."

"You're with pup."

"I'm aware."

I wandered toward him. I was angry at him and scared for his safety, but I was also captivated by my mate's resolve, bravery, and commitment to his new pack.

He had called the pack his family.

I whined as I approached him.

I wanted to touch him.

Our fingers met first—and entwined. Adam grasped my hand and guided it to his belly. He pressed my palm against our pup's temporary home.

"He's safe in there," Adam said.

"He?"

"I suspect we will be having ourselves a stubborn, opinionated Omega male."

"I love that." I stroked Adam's face from cheekbone to chin as I gazed at him, enthralled by the reality that he was carrying our pup.

I took in every feature of his face.

He was so beautiful.

Beautiful and fierce.

"I love you," I whispered to him and nuzzled his cheek. I moved my hand from its place on his belly and embraced him, so our pup was protected between us.

He leaned into my nuzzling and reciprocated, brushing his cheek back and forth over mine. He whined and kissed my jawline. "I love you too, Alpha."

The howl came out of nowhere. One second it was building in my belly, the next it was erupting from my chest. My craving to shift was strong, to increase my vocalization.

Adam harmonized alongside me.

Clear and strong.

We were the Alpha and Omega leaders of the East Creekside pack.

The rest of the pack joined in, filling the valley with sound. Whatever arrangement Bryant had made with the West Creekside pack, they wouldn't be able to rival our leadership.

I touched my nose to his. "We have some time before we expect them."

Adam whimpered, clutched my chin, and closed his mouth over mine; a frenzied wolf chasing his prey. I hauled him away from his truck and up the steps to the front door.

"I'll keep an eye on things," Jonas said as we passed by him.

We were headed down the hall to my bedroom to affirm our devotion. We had declared our love for one another. His words echoed in my mind. We were ours. I longed for that connection with him that would have our thoughts and words meet. To be entirely intimate with him.

"My Omega," I whispered. Early on, I had sensed what Adam would be waiting for. Over the past 10 days, I could have claimed him many times over. I was ready but I knew he wasn't. Adam's ex-mate had claimed him but never told him he loved him. How anyone could be so blind as to not see what an incredible and loving wolf Adam was … was beyond me.

"My Alpha." Adam rocked in my arms as we moved across the bedroom to the bed.

He sat on the edge of the bed as I stripped off my clothes. He ran his hand from my chest to my belly, raking his fingers through my thick dark hair.

My cock was already hard for him.

Adam stripped off his shirt, wrapped his arms around my waist, tugging me close, and kissed my chest. He looked up at me and smiled.

"I love you," he said.

I brushed my hand through his hair. "And I am honored to love you too, Omega."

Adam fussed with his pants, dispensed with them, and shuffled up to the head of the bed. I met him there and descended on his mouth as I stretched out on top of him.

His legs were immediately wrapped around my waist, holding me to him.

We couldn't get close enough to each other.

I nuzzled the scented spot behind his ear. "I want to be yours," I whispered.

"And I yours," he responded, starting the ceremony. Soon

we would each be claimed by the other and joined together for a lifetime. I needed to fill him with my seed again first.

Jonas: *"Lucas! They're not waiting!"*

I jerked away from Adam, surprising him. He touched my arm. We didn't have a single second to spare. I leaped from the bed. "They're on the move!"

Adam scrambled from the bed and joined me streaking down the hallway, onto the front porch, and down the steps. He was swift to shift to wolf and took up an ominous stance beside me.

I waited. The leader of the West Creekside pack might want to talk to me.

As expected, Derek, the leader, strolled out of the forest in non-wolf form.

At his side—Bryant, his green eyes staring out from his thick grey fur.

My brother had allowed himself to be claimed by another Alpha.

"Lucas!"

"Derek!" I moved from foot to foot, prepared to shift at a moment's notice. "What do you want? Why are you on our land uninvited?"

Derek took a few steps forward. "You have something my mate wants."

"Your mate?"

Derek reached down and scratched Bryant's head. "Yeah, it was a quick affair. Bonded. Mated—and claimed. He's been very obedient. I want to reward him."

"This is about my Omega."

"Yes. Bryant tells me you didn't want him."

"I changed my mind."

"You challenged and chased off your own brother,

Alpha."

"He wanted to claim my Omega."

"He made a reasonable request. Offered to keep him away from Creekside."

"Adam wasn't available to be claimed." I touched Adam's muzzle. "We're fated."

"Yes, we all heard your song."

I crossed my arms. This request didn't have a solution. I prepared to shift. The bones along my spine crunched and my canines descended. The dragging sensation in my jaw would make it difficult to speak soon. The change to my vocal cords would be next.

"I'm sure I don't have to tell you; I'm not giving up my fated mate."

"Then we have a problem."

I shuddered and shifted. Derek didn't want Adam for Bryant's sake. This was a power move with my brother's affinity for Adam as an excuse. I leaned against Adam's side. I hoped he'd stick close to me. It would be most effective if we fought together.

Jonas ran up to my other side. The rest of East Creekside was out in front of their houses. They'd fight to the death for me and the legacy of our pack.

The scent of six wolves wandering up the driveway caught my attention. I sensed no ill intent from them. They had probably heard the song of love Adam and I had been singing to each other. The one the rest of the pack had joined in on, celebrating our impending claiming.

A claiming ceremony that had been cut short without completion.

They completed their approach.

I knew most of their faces. These were wolves who had

chosen to live life on their own terms, away from pack life. The oldest of the group nudged my muzzle with his nose. I sensed they had only come to congratulate Adam and me. Now they had a decision to make.

Each one would make up their own mind.

The rest of the newcomers crowded around me. Every one of them bowed their head to me, then faced Derek who had shifted to wolf form.

Our numbers had been strengthened.

Bryant was fast on Derek's heels as Derek launched himself across the clearing toward us. I dug my feet in and took off. I checked over my shoulder. Adam was by my side.

Snarling and growling as ferocious as any Alpha.

The rest of the West Creekside pack emerged from the trees and headed straight for the other members of our pack. My focus was on Derek.

Adam went after Bryant.

I lost sight of Adam as I clashed with Derek, ripping, growling, and snarling, teeth seeking tender pieces of flesh that would slow the other down.

Roll, fight—retreat. Then fly at each other again.

The chaotic chatter of the other wolves in our pack was deafening. There were flurries of strategies being shouted, some seeking each other out, and cries for help.

A few weeks before giving birth to twins, even our sister, Carina, was in the mix.

I tried to tune them out.

If I could take down their leader and Adam could take down Bryant, the rest of the West Creekside pack would back down.

On my next brief separation from Derek, I scanned the area around me. I had expected Adam and Bryant to be fighting near us. Other skirmishes were happening close by me, but none were Adam. My heart thundering in my chest made it difficult to think.

I wanted to call out to Adam through a joined connection, find him, and ensure he was safe. Not having that connection pulled at my heart. I backed away from Derek.

I had no idea where Adam was.

I sniffed the air. There was only a lingering scent of him. I whined, hoping he'd hear me. I got no response. No comforting return of his body next to mine. No nudge with his shoulder.

I whined louder.

I'd never felt so desperate.

Derek looked over his shoulder, listening, then turned back to face me. He narrowed his eyes at me, spun, and took off into the trees.

The uninjured members of my pack surrounded me, sniffing and nuzzling me. Jonas was the first to start the howl. A howl of despair. It filled the forest with a haunting sound.

Their Alpha's Omega was missing.

When the song was finished, the pack members began shifting back.

Jonas lay his hand on my shoulder after I shuddered through my shift.

"They've taken him," I said.

"Then we take him back," Jonas replied. "We load the trucks up with guns and head over there. They won't expect a full assault like that from us."

I shook my head. "They won't have taken him back to their houses." I looked around at the small gathering. "I need some of you to attend to the wounded."

I had a decision to make. Either I shifted and tracked

Adam with my pack members in non-wolf form carrying arms. Or we all shifted, enabling us to move faster but leaving us unprotected.

Wherever they were taking Adam, they would likely have weapons.

Me: *"Jonas. Shift or weapons?"*

Jonas: *"This isn't about Bryant wanting Adam, is it?"*

Me: *"No, this has nothing to do with Bryant wanting my Omega. With my fated mate at my side, our pack is strengthened. We become more of a threat."*

Jonas: *"What do you think they'll do with Adam?"*

I shivered. Derek had a reputation. He was a brutal leader. His pack members feared him and whatever retribution the wolves in his inner circle would exact if they stepped out of line.

He wouldn't be kind to my mate.

I nearly crumpled to my knees as dread washed over me.

*My Adam.*

*My love.*

Me: *"I half expect to find Adam dead and discarded along their trail."*

Jonas: *"Then we shift."*

I sent the message out to the rest of the pack. I would take the lead. I knew Adam's scent best. I could pull it from the scents of the other wolves if they decided to split up.

We shifted and took off into the woods.

# Chapter Seven | Adam

I came to, barely conscious, to the feel of my body being dragged across the forest floor. My head throbbed and pain screamed out from my shoulder and ribs. I could smell blood—my own.

The forest streaked by, bashing my body around. Whoever had me wanted to make quick progress. My pack probably wasn't far behind. My Alpha tracking me.

I was still in wolf form. My fur was protecting my skin from the rough ground for now. I struggled and lifted my head. Rocks and sharp twigs dug into my injured shoulder.

I whimpered, catching the attention of one of the non-wolf form males near me. Young, but he was big for his age. Tall with broad shoulders. Over one of those shoulders, a rifle.

"He's awake," he called.

"Good." I recognized the voice of the leader of the pack, Derek. "I want this Omega to suffer. To whine and whimper. To see the world spinning as I string him up and gut him."

*Fuck!*

A rush of anxiety tingled through every inch of my body.

*Fight!*

I struggled against the tension pulling on my back legs. The clink of metal told me I was being hauled by a chain. I spun and dug my front paws into the soil, scrambling.

Derek laughed and kicked me, knocking me back onto my side. Snapping and barking, I made a lunge for his foot, but he pulled it away in time. I let my head rest on the ground.

I'd never felt so weak.

My fur felt wet near my abdomen.

I considered shifting but the chains were so tight around my back feet that shifting to non-wolf would likely shatter my ankles because of the size difference.

One of them was already sending needles of agony up my leg.

My ears pricked up at the sound of Bryant's voice.

"You said I could have him."

Derek stopped walking which brought my hauler to a halt. To Derek's right, I could see Bryant. In non-wolf form, he looked exhausted and furiously annoyed.

Derek pressed a finger to Bryant's chest. "No, I said I was doing this for you. And I am. I'm doing this for you and our entire pack. Lucas will not gain an advantage over me or this pack by having this fated Omega at his side. Not one of this size and strength."

"That's not what we agreed."

"Maybe you only heard what you wanted to hear, mate."

"I'm not your mate."

"Oh, but you are. You let me claim you, remember. You even let me mate with you once. And when we return home, I am going to breed you into the ground until you are with pup."

"I'm an Alpha male … you wouldn't do that to me."

"Oh, yes, I would. Even though you're not capable of carrying pups, you are *my* Alpha male now, and you will obey me. I will take you to my bed and breed with you until I tire of you."

Bryant growled and stormed off, headed along the line of wolves walking ahead. My mind swam with pain as the chain jerked and I was tugged back into motion.

The pace was picked up.

I wanted to feel sorry for Bryant's plight but it's what he had chosen. Teaming up with Derek as his mate looked different from what Lucas and I had. We were destined to be equals.

Bryant wasn't as lucky.

I twisted to look behind us as I caught the scent of my Alpha. Derek's pack must have picked up the scent too, because the one pulling me, dumped the chain and aimed his rifle into the trees.

"Put the Omega in the shed," Derek said.

I peered around as a new set of hands dragged me. In the distance, a derelict hunting cabin. Ahead of me, what looked to be a woodshed. I whined in pain as I was hauled up a short set of steps and in through the door. I was dumped, the door closed—and left there.

The crack of a rifle shot sent me scrambling around the floor of the shed, spinning, and turning, thumping, attempting to see out through openings in the wooden siding. My anxiety kicked up. Something in me slowed it down, though. Survival and terror for the fate of my mate.

*My Alpha!*

*Please don't hurt my Alpha!*

The door swung open.

It was Bryant.

I clambered away from him the best I could. Even in the dim light, I could see I'd left bloody smears all over the floorboards. Bryant was staring at the sharp-smelling mess.

He moved toward me.

I snarled and snapped at him.

"Calm down." He raised both hands. "I'm not going to hurt you."

My lips remained peeled back, a low growl in my throat,

as he touched my back feet and started unwinding the chain from them. When he had released them, I shifted to non-wolf.

My ankles were bloody and raw.

One was definitely broken. I couldn't stand. I pressed my hand to my side. When I drew it away, my palm was covered in dark crimson. I was losing a lot of blood.

I looked at Bryant.

"Bryant, please."

"You were supposed to be mine."

"I was never meant to be yours, Bryant … you know that."

"Lucas didn't want you."

"He was scared, that's all. You know why."

Bryant looked at the floor. I wasn't sure if he was hesitating because I was getting through to him or if he was preparing to leave me in that shed for Derek.

I needed to sway his decision.

"I'm with pup, Bryant."

Bryant jerked his head up. His eyes grew wide as tears filled them.

"A pup."

"Yes."

Bryant narrowed his eyes at me. "Do you love him?"

I released a long breath. "Yes. So much so. And he loves me too."

Bryant tipped his head to one side and closed his eyes. I could see he was fighting to keep his thoughts to himself. Derek must be calling for him. Demanding Bryant return to his side.

Outside, I could hear a terrifying level of chaos happening. Wolves barking, snarling, and fighting. Guns going off, echoing throughout the forest. Running. Orders being shouted.

I searched for the voice of my Alpha.

His scent was near.

"Can you walk?" Bryant asked me.

"No. My ankle is broken, and I've lost too much blood."

This information flustered Bryant. He squatted in front of me, tucked one arm under my knees and the other under my shoulders, and hefted me into his arms.

He peered out through the partially open door, then dashed out through it.

We had only stepped a short way into the trees behind the shed when Lucas appeared in front of us. There was no standoff between them. This had been arranged.

Bryant gently transferred me into Lucas' arms.

Lucas nodded at Bryant.

"Thank you, brother."

"There's no need to thank me." Bryant looked over his shoulder. His new pack must be howling in his mind. He turned back to Lucas. "Just raise your pup to be honorable like you."

"You're always welcome to return … to be part of this pup's family."

Bryant shook his head. "No, I've sealed my fate here with this pack."

"We would take you back."

"You would … Jonas even. Not the rest of the pack."

Lucas hoisted me closer to him. I tucked my face against the side of his neck and inhaled his familiar heady scent. I closed my eyes. My surroundings turned to a dull hum.

I could barely make out what Lucas was saying.

"Derek's pack will never trust you after this. He'll have you killed."

"I won't be staying."

"Brother, please … come home. We'll protect you."

Bryant growled and spun away from us. Even in my state of stupor, I could hear movement coming toward us. "Go," he commanded.

Lucas clung to me and pushed through the undergrowth. The thorns of the branches sliced up my shins and shoulders. My mate pushed on until we reached a clearing.

Then he made a sprint for the trees.

I don't remember much after that. I do remember the jostling motion, the heat of my mate's body, the way he kept telling me to hang on. To not leave him.

My next memory was of Lucas storming up the steps of our home. And the warmth of a blanket being wrapped around me. Then the jarring shudder of Lucas' truck as he sped down the driveway. After that, lights overhead as I was rushed down a sterile, white hallway, humans peering down at me with anxious faces as they asked me if I knew my name.

I GROANED as I clung to a metal rail and tried to roll onto my side. A hand stopped me.

"Adam, don't."

*My Alpha's voice.*

I lay back, opened my eyes, and smiled up at him. There was incredible concern and exhaustion visible in his gaze. I wasn't sure why. I turned my head, scanning the room.

We weren't at home.

"Lucas?" I gripped his arm, trying to recall why I was there. It was obviously a hospital. A human hospital. Not the home of an herbal healer as I'd come to expect when injured.

"Shh … you're all right."

"Why am I here?" I moved my other hand. Something

moved with it. I was horrified to find tubing connected to my arm with a needle and feeding back to a plastic sac hanging from a pole.

Lucas caressed my cheek. "Your side was torn wide open."

I jerked and tried to sit up.

"Our pup!"

Lucas sighed. "The humans aren't trained to scan an Omega male with a posterior uterus, but they've assured me there's no evidence you lost it."

I closed my eyes, searching for a connection. The pup was so young; a telepathic link probably hadn't been established yet. I listened for its heartbeat. It was too soon.

"I would know," I said. "I'd know if he was gone."

Lucas leaned forward and kissed my forehead. "Right now, I'm more worried about you."

"They stitched me up?" I touched my side. It was tender and bandaged. On my left leg, a plastic contraption meant to hold my ankle in place.

"I had to explain why you'd been so viciously attacked by a wild animal."

"The humans know we're feuding?" That was never a good thing. They only tolerated us because we acted civilized. We were always one human uprising away from all being shot.

"I assured the human authorities that we have it under control." Lucas held my hand and brushed his thumb back and forth on my skin. "I know the county sheriff. He trusts me."

"*Do* we have it managed?"

Lucas grunted. "We overpowered Derek's pack near where we found you. Took their guns. A few decided to join us. A few ran. Derek took off—presumably to hunt Bryant down."

"Do you think Derek will find him?"

"Not likely. Derek won't wander too far from his pack. Bryant will head North up into the tundra. There will be plenty of game for him there."

A nervous twitch filled my gut. "Am I in danger?"

"No. Derek won't come after you again. His pack is encouraging a challenger. I don't think West Creekside will be Derek's much longer. The challenger has no issue with us."

I closed my eyes. The conversation was wearing me out. Only one thing more. It was my place as Lucas' Omega to ask questions. To be up to date with the health of the pack.

"Did we lose anyone?" I asked as I set my gaze on Lucas again.

"No. All manageable injuries."

"Except mine?"

"I wasn't taking any chances with you. Human medicine is more sophisticated than ours."

I relaxed on the pillow. "I'm tired."

"I'll let you sleep." Lucas smiled at me. "We can discuss pack politics another time."

I laughed gently. "Oh, goody."

"Rest, Omega." Lucas set the most tender kiss on my lips. I wanted to angle up into it, to taste more of him. Fill my body with his love.

Moving hurt too much.

"I love you," I whispered.

"My love and devotion are yours forever, Adam." He placed his hand on my belly. "You and our pup." He stepped back from my bed. "Jonas is going to come sit with you. I need sleep."

"Of course." I smiled at him. I hated to see him go but I knew he'd be back as soon as he was rested enough. A sleep, a shower, and a feed would do him good.

His welcome scent reached me before he entered the room.

*Jonas.*

*My brother.*

He walked into the room and headed straight for Lucas. He gripped his shoulders and steered him toward the door. "You go ahead, Alpha. I have your Omega protected from these humans."

"I'm trusting you."

"I'll make sure they behave." Jonas gave Lucas a shove toward the door. Before Lucas left, my Alpha mouthed the words, *"I'm yours,"* to me.

It reminded me that we hadn't claimed one another yet.

I fell asleep imagining what that would be like.

To be loved and claimed.

# Chapter Eight | Lucas

I probably shouldn't have vacuumed a third time. The red and blue area carpet in the living room was threadbare as it was. It didn't need extra help from me to fall apart.

I turned off the vacuum and stored it in the closet.

Jonas had volunteered to bring Adam home from the hospital today. I would have, but I had to stay close to the house in case the new leader of the West Creekside pack decided to stop by. His Omega had come by earlier, hinting that his Alpha might find time for me today.

It had been three days since he challenged Derek and won. I could wait for him. Peace was more important than my pride at having to accept someone else's annoyingly slow time schedule.

The scent of my Omega filled my nostrils.

It made my blood hum with pleasure.

I'd never felt love like this before. I had thought my love for my lost chosen mate had been strong. What I felt for Adam was different. A depth of my soul type of love. When I thought about him, my view of the world brightened. My hope soared. My heart knew it had found its home.

I rushed onto the porch and down the stairs. Jonas was helping Adam out of the truck. I took over, supporting Adam as he hobbled along on the boot that supported his broken ankle.

He kissed my cheek as we stood at the bottom of the stairs.

"I'm home," he whispered to me.

"We'll raise our pup and grow old here." In the week Adam had been in the hospital, the staff had scanned him again and found a soft little precious heartbeat safe inside him.

Six weeks from now, we'd be cradling a warm furry bundle.

I lifted Adam into my arms and carried him up the stairs. I headed straight for our bedroom. I had set the room up for him to convalesce. Warm comforters. Pillows to prop him up. A table that extended over the bed, its firm surface covered in drawing paper and colored pencils.

While in the hospital, Adam had drawn a beautiful picture of our home. I had already framed it and hung it in our bedroom. He wanted to work on a picture of Jonas' restaurant *Growlers* next.

He was incredibly talented.

It was a shame he had chosen to become an electrician instead of following his dream of working in graphic arts. I could tell that's where his heart lay.

When he was settled, I sat on the bed beside him. He reached over, clung to my hand, and rested his head on my shoulder.

"I'm glad to be home," he said.

"I'm glad you consider this to be your home."

"How could I not? You're here."

I kissed the side of Adam's head, then placed my hand on his stomach. "The three of us make a home no matter where we are."

"And Jonas."

I laughed. "Okay. And Jonas."

Adam growled softly and nudged my cheek with his nose. "I want to be yours."

I angled back from him. He was in no condition to engage in a claiming ceremony, yet he had started the words to one. "Adam, we're in no rush."

"I don't want to wait. Not being able to reach out to you, and make sure you were safe … was agony, Lucas. I don't ever want to feel like that again. I want us to be intimately one."

"As do I. My heart was shredded into a million pieces not knowing if you were alive."

"Then let's do it." Adam touched my face, then slid down in the bed until he was lying flat and pulled on the neck of his t-shirt until it ripped, exposing his shoulder.

"I want to be yours," he tried again.

It would be unconventional without the mating portion of the ceremony, but we could always revisit that another time. I moved down until we were face to face.

"And I yours," I said.

Adam smiled at me. I loved to see that smile. It meant my Omega felt safe and content. It fulfilled a primal part of my being beyond simply loving him.

I rose on one elbow, hovering over him. I buried my face along his neck on the far side and inhaled his scent. I kissed his jawline and his ear, then down along his throat as he lifted his head.

He whined and whimpered, ramping up my desire for him.

I cruised down to his shoulder with my lips and licked the claiming area. My canines descended, making my gums throb. I raked them along his skin.

He moaned and gripped my arm.

"Claim me, Alpha."

I sank my teeth into him, and he cried out—a mix of pleasure and pain. I swept his blood into my mouth and waited for the hum of an opening connection.

It filled my mind like fireworks.

Adam's hand came to rest on my bicep, and he pushed me away until I rolled onto my back. Gingerly, he layered his chest on top of mine.

He didn't linger. The pain from his wound had to have been intense. A few soft kisses on my shoulder and then he pierced my skin with his teeth.

He growled as he clamped down, sucking.

A soft whoosh joined the fading fireworks in my head. Adam stopped and pulled away from my shoulder. His bloody lips smiled down at me.

Adam: *"Hello, mate."*

A tear rolled down my cheek.

Me: *"Finally ... we're one."*

Adam: *"Forever."*

I kissed him and rolled him gently off me. "Now, you need to rest."

Adam: *"Wake me later with a kiss in my mind."*

Me: *"You're a romantic, aren't you?"* I pushed away from him and climbed off the bed. "Get some sleep and I'll wake you later for dinner."

Adam was asleep before he had a chance to speak, his lips crimson with my blood. He looked like an impressive, oversized angel, his chest rising and falling softly.

I stepped out of the room and closed the door.

"Is he doing all right?" Jonas said, then caught a look at my face. I licked my thumb and brushed it across my lips, then tasted it. Adam's blood was memorable. Its own unique flavor.

Jonas clapped his hands together. "You claimed each other?"

"I was just about to announce it."

"You didn't howl."

I smiled. "Poor Adam … he insisted but he barely made it through."

Jonas furrowed his brow. "I hope you didn't mate with him. He's barely healed."

"No, of course not." I walked toward the kitchen. "We can repeat the ceremony when he's feeling better." I smiled as I pulled a beer from the fridge. I had sent out the message about our *claiming* to the pack. The jubilant sound of the pack howling made it inside our house.

Our pack was whole. Whole and healthy. The leader was mated. His fated Omega claimed. A new pup on the way. Three in fact if you included our sister's twins.

My sire would have been proud of me.

I only wished Bryant was around to partake in our joy.

I wasn't given any time to wonder about that and the impact not having him in the pack would mean. There was a thundering knock on the door, and I groaned. I had sensed him and his Omega coming up the driveway. I had hoped the Alpha leader's itinerary was full for the day.

I checked on Adam in my mind. He was sleeping peacefully.

I swung open the door. "Carl." I extended my hand, and he shook it. We took a moment to inhale each other's scent, fixing it in our minds. "Come." I led the way into the living room.

Carl and his Omega Mark took a seat across from me.

"Can I get you both a beer?" Jonas asked them.

"One for me," Carl said. "Not my Omega. We are suspicious he is with pup."

That was good news. A pack leader with a pup was less likely to start anything with rival packs. The safety of his family unit was more important than territory.

"Congratulations," I said.

"You as well," Carl replied. "I was pleased to hear your Omega survived his experience with my predecessor. And that your pup survived as well."

"Yes, we were very lucky."

Carl lifted the beer Jonas had placed on the coffee table in front of him. "I was surprised to hear you took him to a human hospital. Will you be doing that for the birth as well?"

"Only if we need to. Mama has offered her services with the birth."

"Your family will be in safe hands then." Carl took a long swallow of his beer and set the bottle back on the table. "Down to business now."

"Yes." I was anxious to confirm my hopes for our relationship. We needed to return to a life of peace. A peace our packs had enjoyed for decades.

"I have no intention of crossing into your territory again unless it is for a friendly visit." Carl looked around the room with his hands held out. "Such as this."

"Or if our pups want to have play dates," Carl's Omega Mark added.

That would be very civilized. Our pups would be in the same grade at school. It would be nice if they weren't restricted from becoming friends with each other. Carl was older than me, but his younger brother, Colin, had been my best friend. I was saddened when years back, Colin met his fated mate on a business trip out of state and decided to join her pack.

"Adam and I would be amenable to that."

Carl leaned forward in his chair. "I'd also like to extend an additional heartfelt apology for the pain our pack caused your pack and your family. I trust your injured members are on the mend."

"A few superficial bites and bullet wounds. Our healer is skilled."

Carl nodded and rose to his feet. "Well, I'd say that concludes it."

"Thank you for offering an apology." I reached across the coffee table and shook Carl's hand. "It's accepted. I'm pleased to return to times of peace between us."

"Excellent." Carl headed for the door with Mark following two full steps behind him. Their relationship appeared to be more traditional. I followed and opened the door for them.

"Thank you for stopping by."

Carl looked at Mark. "Perhaps our Omegas could meet in town for tea and compare notes on their pregnancies. Am I correct in that it's the first pup for them both?"

"Yes, it is. I'll pass the suggestion along to Adam."

A small smile lifted one side of my mouth. If Carl knew Adam, it was unlikely he would want my Omega anywhere near Mark. My mate was likely to corrupt Mark with notions of independence, stubbornness, and general disobedience. Many of the things I loved about him.

Jonas joined me at the door as Carl and his Omega made their way down the driveway. "Mark sometimes comes into the restaurant on his own."

"That surprises me."

"He takes art classes at the community center."

"What kind of classes?"

"I want to say watercolors. Mark showed me some of his work. He's good."

"Do you think it's something Adam would be interested in?"

"Not quite the type of art he's used to doing. But mention it to him anyway." Jonas closed the door and headed down the hall toward his room.

A gentle warm shift in my mind made me smile.

Adam was waking.

I climbed onto the bed beside Adam in time for him to open his eyes and see me there. The smile that lit up his gorgeous expressive face made my heart stutter.

He was the Omega of my dreams.

IT WAS TWO WEEKS later when Adam started to show significantly. A round firm belly that required us to find suitable maternity clothing for him. Jeans with a stretchy front. Looser shirts.

Through our joined connection, I was able to catch glimpses of our pup's awakening mind. Everything was all dulled sounds and jiggles when Adam laughed.

Which I tried to make happen often.

Today was a milestone. Adam's bandages were coming off and after taking an x-ray of his ankle, it was decided the boot could be removed as well. As wolves, we heal faster than humans. Adam was weeks ahead of schedule. As soon as we returned home, we both shifted and took off into the forest to simply stretch out Adam's muscles. We were gone for hours.

We came back stumbling naked across the clearing, laughing.

I gathered Adam up in my arms and kissed him, tugging him to me. We danced against each other, swaying and caressing. My cock hardened, pressing against Adam's swelling belly.

"Omega," I whispered.

"My Alpha."

Adam deepened the kiss as he stroked my back, and my hand drifted to his ass, clutching. I pulled him closer as my lust for him built. We hadn't mated since our time together in the cabin.

During Adam's recuperation, I had slipped below the sheets on occasion and endeavored to break Adam's monotony of being confined to bed rest. They were some of my happiest moments; Adam mewling and gasping and gripping my head through the material as he filled my throat.

But I was anxious to reclaim him.

I growled against Adam's throat and ground my throbbing cock against him.

*"Oh, my god, you two!"* Jonas popped into our minds. *"PDA alert! Get the hell into the house!"* We both giggled like a couple of adolescents but heeded Jonas' suggestion.

"Where were we?" Adam ran his fingers into the hair at the back of my head and devoured my mouth as we thudded and banged into walls on the way to the bedroom, turning against each other again and again until we were through our bedroom door.

Adam laughed as we dropped gently onto the bed, him under me, looking up at me with such love and devotion in his eyes. And happiness—intense sublime happiness.

I sighed as I approached his ear with my lips, then nibbled on the tender lobe with my teeth. I sucked the damp flesh into my mouth as Adam arched up beneath me, his thick hard cock riding the crest of his firm belly, the entire area becoming one of my favorite places to be.

I set a row of slow kisses from the base of his throat to just below his sternum. It was there that his once taut, muscled abs had softened. I shuffled down and cupped the lower part of our pup's burgeoning home in both my hands. I kissed my

Omega's belly button and hummed against the skin below it, hoping our pup would become familiar with my sound.

# Chapter Nine | Adam

I gasped, shuddered, and threw my head back in ecstasy as Lucas lifted my legs and encased my seeping cock with his warm demanding mouth. Every bit of suction, swirl of his tongue, and draw of his lips was perfectly designed to bring me pleasure. While I'd been recovering from my injuries, Lucas had spent a fair amount of time down there to alleviate my boredom.

Now with my belly swelling, he was starting to improvise to accommodate the lack of space around my cock. I gripped the bedding in both hands, gathering it into balls. With each descent of my Alpha's mouth, his thumb breached deeper into my wet hole.

I fought against clamping down, wanting him to go higher. Lucas released my cock and kissed my inner thigh. Then the other. Then the steepening rise of my stomach.

My Alpha worshipped me. I could see it in his eyes as he returned to my mouth. As he kissed me, he smoothed his clean thumb across one of my puffy nipples. Gently. They were becoming extremely sensitive. I longed for the feel of our pup drawing nourishment from them.

A tingle in the one he was stroking pulled at my insides.

My thoughts must have strayed into his mind.

I closed my eyes and groaned as Lucas' mouth encased my nipple and sucked softly. I dragged my fingers through his hair, keeping him in place; the sensation, part pinching—part deep ache.

"Oh, Alpha … yes."

Lucas kissed my chest, then nuzzled my other nipple.

"My beautiful, Omega … so ripe and full."

He lifted himself from where he was on the bed, turned me onto my side, and lay down behind me, his chest firm against my back, his hand cupping my belly.

He kissed my shoulder, then up the length of my neck. His breath was heavy on the back of my ear as I reached back for his cock and guided him toward my warmth.

I'd been aching for him for weeks. He'd been insistent on allowing me to fully heal before he mated with me again, though. And trust me, I'd tried my best to entice him.

I closed my eyes and grunted softly. One slow glide forward and my Alpha was seated in me. He moved his hand from my belly to my hip.

I had expected it to feel different, but I was unprepared for the level of increased intensity. Every nerve ending inside me was alight. Each thrust of Lucas' hips had me gasping for breath.

I licked my lips as a howl started from deep within. I knew it would be low and guttural and amplify everything I was feeling from the depths of my soul.

Every sensation—every emotion.

Lucas joined me, his voice a mix of a howl and a rumble. This was between us. The sound barely left our room. I swooned when Lucas' canines skimmed across my shoulder.

"Yes, Alpha," I encouraged.

He hugged me with his one arm, clutching my wrist tight against my chest, and increased the pace of his hips. Each stroke drove his cock higher into me.

Growling and shuddering as he filled me with seed, Lucas' teeth pierced the flesh of my shoulder, claiming me again. I almost became feral; I was so overwhelmed by sensation.

And love.

More than anything, I was overwhelmed by love.

I WAS AWOKEN by Jonas poking around in my mind. I'd made the decision to block everyone else in the pack out of my mind. If something important happened, Lucas and Jonas would tell me.

Jonas: *"Omega ... wake up."*

I rolled over toward the window. It was still dark out. Lucas was sound asleep. Whatever Jonas' message was it wasn't meant for both of us.

Me: *"What is it?"*

Jonas: *"Carina is in labor."*

I sat up and rubbed the heel of my hand against my eyes. I knew what this meant. As a mated Omega, I was expected to be present for the birth. Especially as the pack leader's Omega.

Me: *"I'll be there in a minute."*

I frowned. Carina should have told me herself. It was understandable that she hadn't. I'd only met her amongst the inner chatter of the pack. After the attack by West Creekside, Carina had taken to her bed, the stress of the fight almost causing her to lose her pups. I'd felt guilty for nearly bringing that about and she held animosity toward me for placing her and her pups in danger.

We'd never spoken one-on-one.

After pulling on sweatpants and a t-shirt, I wandered into the kitchen, hoping to have some water before I left. Jonas was sitting at the kitchen table chewing on a raw and bloody beef steak.

He looked awake and wired.

"Why are you still up?" I lifted a glass from the cupboard and turned on the faucet, filling my glass. "You should be in bed. Carina shouldn't have woken you."

"I'm excited about meeting the pups."

I leaned against the counter. "It'll be a while yet." Between the trip to the bathroom and my arrival in the kitchen, I'd contacted Mama who was overseeing the birth of the twins. Carina was whining and pacing, and layering her bed in blankets, but she wasn't pushing yet.

I didn't know much about female birth. It had never interested me as much as hearing stories from the male Omegas with pups. The process was different. The timing—the nuances.

Everything.

"I'd better go." I threw back the entire glass of water. I was always so thirsty. But then as soon as I drank and started walking, I had to pee. I dashed to the bathroom one more time before I headed out into the darkness along the path that led to Carina's house.

The lights were dimmed in the entire house, more so in the bedroom. Only Mama, Carina, and one other Omega were present. I felt a little guilty for not arriving sooner.

Carina was in the middle of the bed on all fours, running through sets of breathing exercises. The same ones Mama had started me practicing. Lucas had been curious as I sat in the middle of our bed and tried to regulate my long intakes and out breaths. It had been difficult to keep a serious face when he had joined me, sat behind me, and rested his chin on my shoulder.

I had passed Carina's Alpha male when I entered the house. He was sitting with two others in the living room. Lucas had told me he didn't want it to be that way for us. That when

I went into labor, he would be by my side. That he would be there when our pup was born.

I sat on a chair in the corner of the room. I wasn't sure what I was supposed to be doing. I folded my hands in my lap. When Lucas' first mate had passed away, he hadn't been in the room. He'd been sitting in the living room like Carina's mate was now. It had nearly killed Lucas, missing the chance to say one last word of love to his mate before they were gone.

I sniffed and wiped a tear from my cheek.

I'd caught the looks of worry on Lucas' face as he watched me. I knew he was terrified. Every step of this pregnancy so far had made him nervous.

Mama: *"Adam."*

Me: *"Yes, Mama."* I rose to my feet and approached the bed. There had been a change in Carina while I hadn't been paying attention.

Mama: *"Breathe with her."*

I sat on the edge of the bed and touched Carina's hand. She raised her head and her Alpha gaze caught mine. My Omega brain wanted to bow to her.

Carina: *"I'm glad you're here."*

Me: *"Yes, sister, of course."*

Carina's contractions began in earnest. I helped her breathe through them all. Before long, two small whimpering pups were piled upon Carina's chest so Mama could tidy up down below.

I petted one and then the other. Furry and perfect, they were both almost brindle like their sire. Carina set their chubby little bodies on the bed and turned onto her side. I watched with fascination as Carina shifted to wolf form and the pups latched onto her pink, milk-filled nipples.

I left the room with Mama and the other Omega to allow

for Carina's Alpha to attend to her. He would care for her until she felt ready to rejoin the pack.

Jonas would have to wait for introductions.

When I crept into our home, there was no sign of Jonas, but Lucas was in the kitchen making two cups of chamomile tea. He poured the boiling water into the cups.

"How was it?" he asked.

I wandered up beside him and put my arm around his waist. I rested my cheek on his shoulder. "To be honest, a little frightening. Not that anything bad happened. Watching Carina and breathing through contractions with her brought home the fact that we'll have a pup in 4 weeks."

"It's hard to believe we've only known each other for five."

I smiled against Lucas' shoulder. "Five weeks ago, I hated you."

"And now we're starting a family."

That made me hum with contentment. The sound of that. *Family.*

It also reminded me that I had a carrier back in my old home who had no idea what had happened to me. And that she must be frantic with worry.

I could either drive toward the city and phone her on my cell phone, or I could make the trek all the way back and visit her. Let her meet my Alpha and feel my belly for herself.

"I want to visit my carrier." I looked into Lucas' eyes to gauge his reaction. He furrowed his brow. "We'll be gone less than a week. There is peace between the two packs, Jonas can be left in charge, and we have plenty of time until the pup is born."

Lucas exhaled long and slow.

"I wouldn't feel comfortable being away from home."

I put my hand on his chest as something occurred to me. "Have you ever been away from Creekside? Have you spent your entire life right here?"

"I've been to Riverton to pick up supplies plenty of times."

"That's not the same. I suspect Riverton is exactly like Creekside."

"I don't know what to expect in a city."

Unlike living in the city, in addition to not having cell phones, Creekside didn't have access to television or streaming services either. Lucas would have no idea what a city was like.

"You'll be with me. You'll be fine."

"I hear cities are noisy."

"We'll buy you earplugs."

"And smelly."

I grinned at him. "You're running out of excuses."

Lucas sighed. "When do you want to leave?"

"Tomorrow?"

"Okay." He kissed my fingers. "Omega, I'm only doing this because I love you."

"And I love you right back for doing it." I burrowed into the hug Lucas pulled me into. My carrier was going to love Lucas. Love how much Lucas loved me.

Simply be thrilled I was in love.

THE DRIVE WAS LONGER than I remembered. Once we reached cell range, I called my carrier. I was right. She had been frantic with worry. I told her I was coming home for a visit and that I had two surprises she was going to love. After scolding me for not calling sooner, she warmed.

On the outskirts of town, I took over driving. It felt strange having the steering wheel so close to my belly. I found myself glancing down at the proximity. I was extra careful as skyscrapers came into view on the horizon and the traffic around us increased in volume.

I took a quick look at Lucas. He was gripping the handle of his door, his face set in a very serious configuration. His eyes were scanning back and forth. He was definitely tense.

I had booked us into a hotel very near my carrier. She lived in a small apartment that didn't have room for us to stay. Lucas found this very odd. Staying somewhere away from the pack.

There were plenty of free spaces to stay amongst the pack members, but I had left them behind without a word of explanation. I doubted I was welcome in any of their homes.

"How long?" Lucas asked.

"Just another 5 minutes."

"Not being able to feel and hear the pack is making me agitated."

"Jonas has everything handled. Plus, he has my cell number. "He'll call if he needs us."

"It's just so quiet. It's given me a knot in my stomach … I feel incredible sadness."

"That's normal."

Me: *"I love you, Alpha."*

Lucas: *"Promise me, you'll fill my head with noise."*

Me: *"I'll do my best."*

Lucas: *"Love you too, Omega."*

Lucas leaned against the window; his face nearly pressed to the glass as we drove down busy streets with tall buildings on both sides of the road. We turned a corner, and my old neighborhood surrounded us. I pointed out the window.

"My elementary school is just down there."

"In the middle of the city?"

"Where else would it be?" I nudged his shoulder. "Down that alley there, I had my first fight in wolf form. It was with an Alpha five years older than me. Got my ass kicked."

Lucas looked at me. "Did you do that often? Get in fights."

"I was an Omega the size of an Alpha with a chip on my shoulder. What do you think?"

"You didn't know your place."

I rested my hand on his thigh. "My place is with someone like you. In a position where I am equal with my Alpha where I can contribute to leading a pack."

"True. You're perfectly suited to it."

I slowed the car and looked out the window at a high tower that was our hotel. I pulled onto the side of the road in front of it. We could unload our bags and then I would park the car.

We walked into a lobby full of humans. Their rotting vegetation scent was overwhelming. I trained my face and didn't wrinkle my nose. Lucas wasn't as successful.

I hadn't experienced Lucas around humans before. Our time together had been so short and packed full of chaos that we had never gone into town together. I knew Lucas was a big guy. He was even taller and broader than me. But next to a human.

He was massive.

People backed away from us as we made our way to the counter. Wolves generally stuck to their own nooks and crannies in the city. We had walked right into the center of the human world.

I approached the man standing behind the counter. He looked me up and down, noticed my belly, and sneered at me. I peeled back my lips at him and showed him my descended canines.

Luckily, Lucas didn't catch the exchange.

"Reservation for Parker," I said to the concierge.

Lucas raised his eyebrows at me. In all the time we had been talking, I had never shared my last name with him. I suppose I should have used Black since we were essentially married by claiming each other if we followed human convention.

The concierge peered at us in silence, then typed on his computer.

"We'll have to charge you an extra pet deposit," he said.

I felt Lucas tense. I lay my hand on his arm.

Me: *"Leave it."*

Lucas: *"That's an absolute insult. What does he think we're going to do?"*

Me: *"They've probably had experience with wolves shifting and trashing the rooms."*

Lucas: *"We wouldn't do that."*

Me: *"He doesn't know that."*

"That's fine," I replied to the concierge. "But I assure you there will be no trouble."

The man didn't look convinced. He handed me a small paper envelope with two suite entry keycards in it. "Room 1412. Up the elevator and down the hallway to the right."

"Thank you." I took the keys and tucked them in my pocket.

Lucas grabbed both of our bags and followed me to the elevator. He tipped his head to one side, hesitating at the doors. "Can we take the stairs?"

"I'm 4 weeks pregnant. I'm not going up fourteen flights of stairs. Get in."

He was reluctant, but stepped in and gripped the handrail

tightly as the elevator carried us to the fourteenth floor. I smiled. He was holding his breath.

The room was standard. Except, I had requested a room with a king-sized bed like the one we had at home. Even it barely contained us.

Lucas wandered straight to the window.

"We're so high," he said.

I stepped up behind him, wrapped my arms around his waist, and laid my cheek against the back of Lucas' head. My belly pressed into the small of his back. "Does it bother you?"

Lucas shook his head. "No. I can see the entire city from up here."

"I'd like to lie down before we head to my carrier's for dinner. I just have to move the car." I headed to the bathroom first. My bladder was screaming to be emptied. Lucas was lying down when I re-entered the room. I decided the car could wait a few minutes.

I cuddled up next to him, tucked into the crook of his arm, my face on his chest.

"Are you nervous?" I asked.

"To meet your carrier? Not really. It'll be interesting to meet a female Alpha. The only one I know is my sister. And I know how much of a handful she can be."

"Her name is Cynthia, by the way. She prefers if you call her that."

"You don't call her Mom in front of humans."

"No, she never liked that."

"Our parents had us call them Dad and Papa."

I laughed. "I called my sire Sir."

"He was that strict?"

"Didn't do much good. I was a bit of a wild child."

"I'm not surprised. You've told me some interesting

stories about your youth."

I sighed. "I'm not sure I can sleep. I'm excited to see Cynthia."

"Can we go early? Help prepare dinner?"

I lifted my phone and texted Cynthia. The answer was positive.

"She says she'd love that."

"I want to change into something nicer." Lucas removed himself from the bed and started digging in his duffel bag. One I had lent him. He didn't even have one of his own.

When we left, we were both dressed respectably. There had been a few moments of making out between changes of clothes. It was hard for us to keep our hands off each other.

We were giggling as we entered Cynthia's building. Lucas hadn't been able to stop himself from commenting on the horrendous state of the sidewalks and roadways. They were like a patchwork quilt of concrete and asphalt and planks of plywood from the sidewalks to the road.

I was used to it.

He hadn't been impressed about angling through crowds of homeless people either. He couldn't understand why the city allowed it. Why everyone wasn't housed. I had to explain to him that humans weren't like wolf packs. They weren't as diligent about taking care of each other.

The giggling stemmed from horrendous smells coming from a back alley near my carrier's apartment. The faces Lucas had made sent me into hysterics. Apparently, my laugh was contagious to Lucas. He hugged me, grinning, as we packed into a small closet elevator.

Cynthia would have sensed an Alpha coming up the elevator with me, but I wanted to surprise her anyway. I made Lucas stand to one side of the door out of sight.

The expression on Cynthia's face was everything I'd hoped it would be. My carrier loved me. She immediately hauled me into her arms—gasped—and took a step back and looked down.

"You're with pup!"

"4 weeks." I grinned at her then motioned for Lucas to join me. I linked my arm with his and leaned my head against him. "And this is my fated mate—my Alpha. My Lucas."

"Fated, hey?"

Her gaze was analytical, taking in every contour of Lucas. She inhaled deeply. Even stepped close to Lucas to pull in a full breath. She was all Alpha.

She stepped back and crossed her arms. "You love my Adam?"

Lucas cleared his throat. "With my entire heart."

"His last mate never loved him."

"I assure you that is not the case with me."

"You'll care for him and the pup?"

"They're my family and part of my pack. Both are safe with me."

"What's your position in your pack?"

"I'm the leader."

One of Cynthia's eyebrows arched. "That suits Adam's temperament well. He was born to lead. You'll of course treat him as your equal."

"He *is* my equal."

That answer seemed to satisfy Cynthia. She waved us into the living room and closed the door. "We can eat early. I'm sure you're famished from the drive."

Lucas and I followed Cynthia into the kitchen. She had my favorite meat on the chopping block. An entire cage of beef ribs. "Wash the blueberries and set up the table, please."

I directed Lucas to sit in the dining room. There wasn't enough room in the kitchen for all three of us. I dumped the berries into a colander and rinsed them in the sink.

Everything was exactly where it had been my entire life. I lifted a chipped blue bowl down from the cupboard and dumped the blueberries into it. I remembered chipping that bowl. I had been tossing marbles into it to hear the clink noise. My sire had been furious.

"Quail's eggs," Cynthia said.

She was putting on a full meal. I couldn't wait for Lucas to try everything. He'd likely only had chicken eggs and I wasn't sure how plentiful blueberries were in Creekside.

After everything was arranged on the table, I took a seat next to Lucas.

I started with a handful of blueberries. It had been a while since I'd had any. Lucas watched me then tried some. I was right, they probably didn't have blueberries in Creekside. Likely only huckleberries that could be harvested from the forest. These were sweeter.

The ribs were next. All three of us dug in, growling, and snarling as we attacked the meat. It was nice not having to wait to feed. As an Omega, I'd been made to sit as a child until my parents were finished. Now I was a leader of the East Creekside pack. I'd never have to wait again.

I reached for some eggs, picked up three, and tossed them into my mouth. The smooth, rich flavor combined with the crunch brought back memories of holiday meals.

Lucas appeared to like them. He ate 10.

Satisfied and cleaned up, we retired to the living room to relax. I'd help Cynthia with the dishes when she moved to head to the kitchen. For now, we were going to snooze in front of the electric fire. All three of us nodded off for over an hour.

"Tell me about how you support my Adam," Cynthia started after waking.

"I have an electrical business," Lucas replied.

"Like Adam's?"

"No, slightly larger. There are four of us … or there were. Now, there are three."

"What happened to the fourth?"

"My brother, Bryant." Lucas looked down at his hands. "We had a falling out."

"Amid a pack?"

I put my hand on Lucas'. "He tried to claim me, Cynthia. Obviously, that wasn't going to happen. He took it too far and separated himself from the pack."

"That's unfortunate. Family is important."

"I still have my brother and sister. Jonas and Carina."

"You're very fortunate. Adam was an only pup."

"Not anymore. Jonas in particular considers Adam to be his brother."

That made me blush. Especially remembering I had almost rutted with Jonas because I was trying to get back at Lucas for saying he wanted to gut me.

That would have been an embarrassingly insane thing to have in our past.

It was bad enough that we had kissed.

"I'm so pleased. Excuse me a moment. Dishes." Cynthia rose from her seat, and I followed her to the kitchen. She started washing. I grabbed a tea towel to dry.

"You seem very happy," she said to me.

"He is incredible, Cynthia. So gentle and caring and loving. I couldn't have asked for a better mate. He's everything I had hoped I'd have someday."

"So, he really does treat you well."

"I'm precious to him and he lets me know it."

"Yes, I can see that in his eyes when he looks at you." She dropped the cleaning sponge and pulled me into a hug. "I am so pleased you found him … your fated mate. You're very lucky."

"I know." I tugged her tightly to me. Her scent was so familiar. It made me homesick. I went back to drying. "I wonder what would have happened if I hadn't left here."

"You would have found another chosen mate. Claimed and with pup, I'm sure."

"Not with the intense love I have now, though."

"No, probably not."

I dried the last dish and put it in the cupboard. "I think we'll go. I want to take Lucas for a walk down by the water. It's a beautiful clear night for it."

"Sounds perfect. Be sure to bundle up. It's cold down there."

We said our goodbyes and then I directed Lucas down the street toward the ocean. There was a lovely walkway along there. It was still early in the evening, so it was packed—mostly by humans. Occasionally, you'd catch the scent of a wolf or two. Maybe even a family of them.

One approaching scent had me recoiling and gripping Lucas' arm.

"What's the matter?" Lucas stopped our progress and turned me to face him.

"Trent," is all I said as butterflies went insane in my stomach.

"Your ex?"

"Yes, he's here. He's coming toward us."

The scent with Trent was familiar. It was the scent of a wolf he had told me was his new office assistant. Trent had come home smelling of him for a good two months before he left me.

I'd never met him.

I hadn't met his fated mate either.

My breath caught as Trent stopped in front of us. The Omega wolf with him was lean and much shorter than him. At his side a pup who looked to be about two months old.

I swallowed as my face flushed.

It couldn't be.

"Adam," Trent said. "Didn't think you lived around here anymore."

"I don't. I live about 7 hours drive away. We're visiting my carrier."

"Ah." Trent's gaze went from my belly to Lucas back to my belly and then to my face. He cocked his head and pointed at Lucas. "Who's this with you?"

I felt my hackles rippling beneath my flesh. I hadn't liked his tone. Near the end, Trent started being condescending toward me. Speaking to me like I was a cowering Omega.

I put my arm around Lucas' waist to calm myself.

"My fated Alpha. The leader of my pack. My claimed mate. Lucas."

"And the pup is yours, I assume," Trent said to Lucas.

Lucas' lips peeled back, and he growled. "Who else's would it be?"

"Not sure. When I first met Adam, he was loose with his choices of rut."

Lucas stepped toward Trent. I grabbed his arm.

Me: *"He's not worth it."*

Lucas: *"He insulted my Omega."*

Me: *"And I can look after myself."*

I pointed at the pup. "Is she yours, Trent?"

Trent crossed his arms. I was about to catch him in something I suspected he would have rather kept from me. He'd certainly managed to keep it out of the pack's inner conversation.

The leader had likely come down on him hard when the pup was discovered.

"Yes," Trent replied. "But you need to understand, Daniel is my fated mate."

Lucas gripped my hand—tightly. He had just completed doing the math in his head. In addition to carrying the scent of Daniel on him when Trent came home from work, I had picked up the scent of mating on him. I assumed it was us. We mated a lot. Every day.

I had discounted the scent of mating on Daniel. I assumed he had a mate.

What Trent had done was unheard of. Claimed mates didn't stray outside the relationship for any reason. I clung to Lucas' arm. Tears were threatening to spill.

"So … the pup is yours?"

"She is," Trent replied.

I slammed a hand on Lucas' chest as he burst forward. His growl was one of an Alpha leader about to put a disrespectful lesser Alpha in his place.

Me: *"Don't. He doesn't matter enough to me."*

Lucas: *"You're hurting."*

Me: *"Can we go back to the hotel and talk about it there? I need your arms around me."*

Lucas: *"Can I hunt him down later?"*

Me: *"Lucas, stop. Let's go ... please."*

Lucas surged at Trent and Trent stepped back, reluctant fear in his eyes. My Alpha wasn't someone you wanted to take on. There were few Alphas who could fight him and win. With me by his side, we made formidable mates. If we decided to strike, Trent and Daniel didn't stand a chance against us. We knew better than to shift in the middle of crowds of humans, though.

"You're a despicable wolf who doesn't deserve a pack," Lucas growled at Trent. "They should have chased you away. You and your Omega and your illicit pup."

Lucas grunted and nodded at me. I'd been moving away from the entire situation. I needed to be out of there. Seeing the wolf I used to love in a family unit, aside from the fact they should be lone wolves, and Lucas was telling them so … I wanted to run before my temper got the better of me. Like Lucas, I wanted to hunt Trent down later. Instead, I knew I needed to walk away.

We hurried down the street back to the hotel.

Once in the room, I crashed on the bed and let the agonizing sorrow pour out of me in the form of wails and tears. Lucas lay beside me and patiently waited me out.

I crawled into his open arms when I started to slow down, sniffling against his shirt.

"I loved him so much," I said.

"I know you did."

"He cheated on me. How could he do that? I was so devoted to him. We had claimed each other. We were supposed to live a lifetime together."

"Trent made an obscene decision when he found his fated mate."

"Why didn't he just bring Daniel into our family like he's supposed to?"

"Maybe his Omega pressured him."

"Did you see Daniel's stance and size? He wouldn't pressure anyone. It was Trent's choice."

"You said you suspected he never loved you. Cynthia agrees."

I rubbed the bridge of my nose against Lucas' neck and played with his thick chest hair. I loved to run my lips through it. I closed my eyes. I was trying to distract myself.

"Is there something wrong with me?" I asked.

Lucas shifted away from me and gazed down at my eyes. "Why would you say that?"

"Trying to figure out why he cheated on me."

Lucas brushed his fingers through my hair. "You're perfect in my eyes. If anything, you were too much wolf for Trent. You needed a strong Alpha who appreciated your independence."

I kissed his neck. "I was destined to find you."

"I think so."

I smoothed my hand from Lucas' chest to his stomach.

"Show me, Alpha. In human terms … I need you to make love to me."

I hummed as Lucas shuffled down to be face-to-face with me and took my mouth. Every desirous surge, every low growl, every kiss covering my skin … it was perfection.

Lucas was my home.

My fated mate.

My forever love.

# Chapter Ten | Lucas

The next 4 weeks crawled by. Adam's belly grew even rounder, and he complained a lot about his feet being swollen and his back hurting. I rubbed both whenever I got the chance.

Like I was doing now. Adam was sitting on the sofa, feet up on a stool and I was squirting lotion into my hands and massaging his feet. Adam had spent the entire morning cleaning the kitchen. The day before that had seen him reorganizing our closet and dressers.

I couldn't count the number of times he had reorganized the nursery.

"Lucas." Adam jumped, his hand on his belly. "Come feel."

I quickly abandoned my post, sat on the sofa beside him, and lay my hand where his had been. There was definite movement. Squirming and tossing.

The sensation brought me so much hope. I could see our family growing beyond this pup. Adam was so beautiful like this, round and happy. He loved being with pup. We had talked about adding more to our brood when the time was right. My heart was so full of joy.

"I'm close," Adam said. "The pup has shifted. I feel heavy lower down." He leaned forward and kissed me. "I also feel like mating with you—badly."

"Right now?" I looked across the room at Jonas. He was reading a book. We'd get a few sly looks from Jonas if we bundled off to the bedroom in the middle of the day.

I decided I didn't care. I rose from the sofa and held out my hand to help Adam stand.

"Your wish is my command," I said.

Adam giggled. I loved when he did that. It was in such contrast to his large stature. I helped him lumber down the hall and assisted him in removing his clothes.

He was so big with pup that the easiest tasks were difficult for him.

I stripped and joined him on the bed. He had remained on his knees. Laying on his back had become painful. I stroked Adam's back as he straddled my hips. His belly pressed to my stomach as he leaned down and kissed me. A long hungry kiss that told me everything I needed to know.

My Omega was strong, and he was going to make it through this.

I caressed his spine, then moved to his ass, clutching handfuls.

Adam groaned into my mouth.

I switched to finding his cock between us. It took some digging, but I uncovered his thick hard shaft. I stroked it slowly as Adam undulated his hips.

I felt a spatter on my chest. I moved my hand to his nipple. It was wet. He'd started leaking milk a few days ago. He was close. It drove Adam wild when I sucked on them.

Adam released my mouth and put one hand on my chest. He used his other hand to guide my cock inside him. He threw his head back as he sunk onto the full length.

"Oh … Alpha."

He groaned as he rode me, his howl becoming louder and louder. There was no way Jonas would be oblivious as to what we were up to. I smirked and joined his vocals.

On the next descent, a wash of warmth flowed over my

hips, down my balls, and between my legs. Adam stopped moving, a panicked look on his face.

"I think my water just broke."

I sat up and put my hands on his waist.

"What do we do?"

"First, I get off you." Adam rolled off me and looked at the blankets. They were soaked. "We're going to need to change the bedding."

"I can do that. You contact Mama, Carina, and whoever else you want here."

"Can Jonas be here as well?"

I wrinkled my brow at him. "He's not mated."

"You said whoever I want."

I gazed at his anxious face. Even uncertain, he was gorgeous; his beautiful eyes staring at me. I knew it from early on. That I was willing to give Adam anything he wanted.

He was my forever.

My entire life.

My pure love.

# Chapter Eleven | Adam

I took Lucas' lack of rebuttal as his agreeing to my request. I contacted everyone and soon our bed was remade, and the bedroom felt like it had too many wolves in it.

I rearranged the bedding. Sat in the middle of it, then rearranged it again. I had an urge to make it perfect for my pup. Then the contractions started. Hot pokers of sensation and a clenching deep inside caught me off guard. I gripped Lucas' arm. I'm sure I was leaving crescent-shaped marks in his flesh, but he didn't complain. He exhaled long and slow next to my ear.

He was reminding me to breathe. I was ready for the next contraction. I used the technique I had been practicing for weeks. Not sure if it reduced the pain but it gave me something else to focus on and that was welcome. The need to go on my hands and knees overwhelmed me.

I did what my body told me to do. Mama's fingers touched my hole and felt around. I was in too much pain to be embarrassed.

"When you feel like pushing, Adam, go right ahead. You're ready."

My back swayed as the next contraction ripped through me. I moved my legs further apart as my belly tensed. I looked up. Lucas was sitting on the bed in front of me. He leaned forward, covered my hands with his, and kissed me. He lifted a hand and stroked my cheek.

"You've got this, Omega. I love you."

I was about to say something, but a desperate urge overtook me, and my attention was drawn away from Lucas. The need to push was incredible.

I bore down.

"That's it, Adam," Mama said.

It felt like forever, pain and pushing. Finally, the burn of my hole being stretched ripped through me. More than I'd ever been stretched before. Then release. I knew the pup was out. I lowered myself to the bed and turned over onto my back. The room seemed hazy.

Lucas leaned down and kissed me then paid attention to what was happening at the end of the bed. Mama had a towel, and she was rubbing our pup vigorously with it. Jonas was standing near her. My new brother blew a few short breaths into our pup's nostrils and Mama kept rubbing.

Tears came to my eyes as soft whimpering sounds filled the room. Gingerly, Jonas took our pup and approached the side of the bed.

I snuffled in a breath and tears streaked my cheeks as Jonas set our pup on my chest. I clung to its chubby little body so it wouldn't roll off me.

"It's an Alpha male," I said after inhaling his scent.

"Oh, goody." Lucas laughed and kissed my forehead.

"And he's big," Jonas added.

"He'll be like his sire." I reached back and cupped Lucas' face. "We did it."

He kissed my cheek. "You did it."

Our little pup wiggled on my chest. I moved him up and he latched on hard to my nipple. I felt a strange drop behind it, but I didn't feel the need to shift. I only had one pup. I preferred to hold him like this. As his fur dried, it felt soft beneath my fingers. I inhaled his entire essence.

Lucas lay beside me, and I set my head on his shoulder. My mate petted our pup and hummed a tune I'd never heard before. This was the most content I had ever been in my life.

I closed my eyes as our pup sucked greedily. I snuggled against Lucas and breathed in their combined scent. This was it. This is what I'd always wanted.

A wolf who loved me.

And a family.

Did you love this story? Do you want to read about Jonas and his love story?

Look for ***Jonas' Alpha*** by JT Fader
An MM Wolf Shifter MPreg Romance

# About the Author

JT Fader is an alternate pen name for Leigh Jarrett (she/he), allowing Leigh to explore their love of MM+ paranormal and fantasy stories by creating their own worlds.

In their hometown of Victoria, BC, Canada, Leigh can be found nestled up with their fabulously supportive wife and trusty laptop or enjoying the wondrous Vancouver Island outdoors.

To stay up to date with JT Fader's new releases and promos, check out their JT Fader Fantasticals website at www.jtfader.com.

You can also find Leigh on Bluesky.

www.ingramcontent.com/pod-product-compliance
Lightning Source LLC
LaVergne TN
LVHW091008080826
845145LV00003B/1174